# THE ENTROPY
TANGO

# The Entropy Tango

## by M. Moorcock

1. The Entropy Tango. At the Time Centre. The Birthplace of Harlequin.

2. Pierrot on the Moon. Harlequin's Courtship. Columbine's Song.

3. Pierrot's Song of Positive Thinking. The Nature of the Catastrophe. Through the Megaflow. Plays its own Tune. The Roof Garden and Columbine's Carol.

4. Every Gun Plays its own Tune. Pierrot in Harlequin. Transformed Columbine's Reconciliation.

5. Harlequin Pierrot and Song of Entropy Columbine's. Tango crepine Lament.

_Hermann._

_Rosinsky._

_Der alte Moor._

Characters:

Nestor Makhno
Major Nye
Catherine
Jerry
Frank
Sebast
Mary
Col.

Una Persson
Mrs Cornelius
Cornelius
Cornelius
Auchinek
Mo Collier
Pyat.

o

# MICHAEL MOORCOCK

# THE ENTROPY TANGO

## A Comic Romance

Pictures by Romain Slocombe
Lyrics by Michael Moorcock

**NEW ENGLISH LIBRARY**
Hodder & Stoughton

**For Pete Pavli**
*(who did most of the music)*

Design Tim McPhee

Copyright © 1981 by Michael Moorcock
First published in Great Britain by
New English Library 1981
NEL Paperback Edition 1987

**British Library C.I.P.**

Moorcock, Michael
    The entropy tango : a comic romance.
    I. Title
    823'.914[F]          PR6063.059

ISBN 0 450 05663 5

---

Printed and bound in Great Britain for
Hodder and Stoughton Paperbacks, a
division of Hodder and Stoughton Ltd.,
Mill Road, Dunton Green, Sevenoaks,
Kent (Editorial Office: 47 Bedford
Square, London, WC1B 3DP) by
Cox & Wyman Ltd., Reading.

# Contents

# List of Illustrations

# INTRODUCTION

# Entropy Tango

My pulse rate stood at zero
When I first saw my Pierrot
My temperature rose to ninety-nine
When I beheld my Columbine

Sigh, sigh, sigh . . .
For love that's oft denied
Cry, cry, cry . . .
My lips remain unsatisfied
I'm yearning so for my own Pierrot
As we dance the Entropy Tango!

I'll weep, weep, weep
Till he sweeps me off my feet
My heart will beat, beat, beat,
And my body lose its heat
Oh, life no longer seems so sweet
Since that sad Pierrot became my beau
And taught me the Entropy Tango

So flow, flow, flow . . .
As the rains turn into snow
And it's slow, slow, slow . . .
As the colours lose their glow . . .
The Winds of Limbo no longer blow
For cold Columbine and her pale Pierrot
As we dance the Entropy Tango!

## At the Time Centre

Calling in and calling out
Crawling through the chronosphere
Will all members please report
To their own centuries
Where they will receive instructions
As to how to progress

This is an emergency signal
To all chrononauts and
Members of the Time Guild
Mrs Persson calls a conference
Code-name Pierrot—code-name Harlequin
Come in please—this is Columbine

Come in please, this is Columbine
Come in please, this is Columbine
Come in please, this is Columbine
Come in please, this is Columbine
Columbine calling,
Calling
Calling out . . .


## The Birthplace of Harlequin

In this ancient time-fouled city discredited gods do brood
On all the imagined insults which down the aeons they've
    received
It is a place of graves and here dreams are destroyed
Dreams are brought from all the corners of the world
To be crushed or ripped or melted down
Into a healthy cynicism
Here are tricksters born
And fools divested of enchantment

This is where Pierrot is killed
And from his flesh Harlequin created
To race across the world, laughing at nothing,
Laughing at everything
Laughing at his pain,
Laughing at the tired gods who bore him
Here in this city, this city of shades,
This city of irony bereft of imagination
This city of suppression
This city of pragmatism
Where the jesters weep
And the tricksters scheme
Parading in motley
Too afraid to scream,
Too wary to acknowledge love
Unless love's made a game.
A game which they can win.

Here, in this city of swaggering fantasticos, of calculated
     gallantry
Was Harlequin the Trickster born, to go about the world,
     to win
To attract; to display an easy cleverness; to lie and
     to deceive
To show what shallow things are dreams, and promises
     impossible to keep
And should he meet with frankness, unashamed honesty
Back to this city Harlequin may flee
To be replenished, armed afresh by his weary masters,
The gorgeous gods of disharmony . . .

# 1. FOR ONE DAY ONLY: TWO MIGHTY EMPIRES CLASH

*Greta Garbo is here seen in the climax scene of "Queen Christina"
after she has forsaken her throne and is sailing away with her dead
lover . . . one of the greatest performances of her career, in a story and
settings which are sombre and admirably suited to her strong
dramatic powers.*

Shots from Famous Films, No. 19, issued by Gallagher
Ltd, c. 1937

"I STILL BREED and buy a little, but I rarely, these
days, kill." Balancing a pink gin in his thin hand Major
Nye settled into the light-blue plush and pulled a
photograph from his top pocket. Behind him was a wide
observation window. He turned to glance through the
clouds at what could be Transcarpathia below. There were
only four passengers in the airship's lounge and two of
them spoke no language known to him, so he was anxious
to keep Mrs Persson nearby. As she approached, he said:
"What do you make of this couple?"

It was too hot. Una Persson regretted her Aran turtle-
neck, and she tugged a little at the top so that her pearls
clicked. "Ukrainians." She smiled at them. They were
shy. "They'll probably have Russian."

"Russki." The woman responded with an alacrity
which dismayed her thick-set husband. "Da." She wore a
mixture of national dress (blouse and boots; a brown suit of
the rather severe cut favoured east of Warsaw). He wore
motley: a short red leather overcoat, tweed trousers, two-
tone shoes.

"Then they're anarchists." Major Nye looked curiously
at the pair before finishing his gin. "Do you think they'll
last?"

Una was amused. They were probably rich emigrants.
"What's the alternative? Bolshevism?"

"Jolly good." Major Nye was also feeling the heat. He
adjusted the left sleeve of his uniform jacket. "Do you
hunt, Mrs Persson? At all?"

"Not seriously."

Nodding at Una, perhaps embarrassed, the Ukrainians replaced their empty glasses on the bar. They offered a muted 'Dasvedanya' to the steward, and climbed up the open oak staircase to the main deck.

"Another half-an-hour and we'll be in Prague." Major Nye was regretful. He had been glad to find an acquaintance aboard. "Have you someone waiting for you? From the Consulate?"

"Do you know Prague?"

"Not since the war." Major Nye smiled like a wistful conspirator. "I change in Dublin for Toronto." He had come from Hong Kong, with a Bradshaw's under his arm, hopping ships after he had missed the *Empress of Canada* on her weekly express run. By taking this flight via China and the Russian Republic he had actually saved himself several hours, since the *Empress* followed an All-Red Route established by sea-going vessels in the century's early years. Now, more than four decades later, big British airships might still moor at aerodromes built on sites of ancient coaling stations. But the Air Ship *Lady Charlotte Lever* belonged to E&A Lines who were concerned less with national prestige than with international competition. Built ten years before, in 1938, she had been one of the first so-called 'China clippers', lifting 31,000 tons and capable of almost 200 mph with a following wind. She stopped at only two British ports, making a six-day round-trip from Nagasaki, via Seoul, Peking, Samarkand, Tiflis, Kiev, Prague, Brussels and Liverpool, to Dublin; challenging the Russian, German and American lines who had previously dominated this territory. Major Nye felt unsafe in her. He preferred more stately, old-fashioned craft.

Mrs Persson sat on the opposite couch.

"I was hoping for a few days leave." Major Nye passed her the photograph. It showed an elderly grey being led from its stall by a smiling, plump young woman. "That's my horse, Rhodes. My daughter, Elizabeth. She runs the stable now. Near Rye. Poor old chap. He's dying. I wanted to be with him.''

She was touched. She returned the photograph. ''A fine animal.''

''He was.'' Major Nye stroked his white moustache with the tip of a nicotine-stained finger. ''Tempus fugit, eh? To the best of us.'' His pale eyes stared hard out of the airship as if he willed back tears.

Una rose. ''I'll have to leave you, I'm afraid. Bags.''

''Of course.'' He stood to attention. ''We'll doubtless meet again. That's the Service. Here today and gone tomorrow.''

''Or vice versa.'' Una shook hands. She brushed the short chestnut hair from her face. ''Good luck in Canada.''

''Oh, it's nothing serious, I'm sure.''

When she had left he realised he still held Rhodes's photograph. He tucked it into a top pocket which he firmly buttoned. Moving between empty chairs, glass in hand, he straightened his jacket, looking behind the bland barman at the mirror. As he set his glass on mock tortoiseshell the ship gave one of those peculiar shudders which usually meant unexpected wind resistance and the glass clicked against a chrome railing before Major Nye's bony fingers could close on it. The lounge darkened. They sailed through heavy cloud and the sun and land had been completely obscured. The steward prepared a new drink.

''Not long now, sir, before we go down.''

## 2

*ESTONIA obtained her independence in 1918. The colours of her distinctive national flag, a horizontal tricolour: Blue for the sky, mutual confidence and fidelity; black for the nourishing soil and the dark past of the country; white for the winter, hope for the future . . .*
National Flags and Arms, No. 16, issued by John Player and Sons, c. 1937

''CAN THIS, AFTER all, be the Golden Age?'' Una turned from the first floor window and the bleak Notting

Hill street. She had arrived in England less than three hours ago and had come directly here, hoping to find her lover Catherine, but only Catherine's mother had been in.

"I could do wiv a bit of it," said Mrs Cornelius, mopping sweat, "if, o' course, there's some ter spare." She laughed and looked at the clock. "Sovereigns." On the wireless, briefly, an announcer spoke of chaos in the outskirts of Toronto, but Mrs Cornelius stretched a fat arm and turned the knob to find Ted Heath and his Music who were half-way through *Little Man You've Had A Busy Day.* "Thass an old one." She was nostalgic. "When did that come art? Four? Five years ago? Makes yer fink." She returned to her horrible armchair and lowered herself into it, magazines and newspapers rising and falling around her as if she sank back into some polluted sea. "Bin abroad agin, 'ave yer, love?"

"Here and there," said Una equably. She felt both terror and affection for Catherine's mother. The woman seemed to maintain an ageless decrepitude, utterly at one with her preferred environment. The paint on her face might have been put on that day or ten years before and was flaking to exactly the same degree as the paint on her woodwork. "Had a holiday this year, Mrs C?"

"Nothin' ter speak of. We went ter 'Astings, ther Kernel an' me, fer Easter. It pissed darn." She spoke of her boyfriend, 'the old Pole', who ran a second-hand-clothes shop in Portobello Road. "Spent the 'ole time on ther bleedin' pier. When we wasn't in ther pub." She raised her tea to her lips. "'*E* was dead miserable, o' course. But *I* enjoyed meself."

"That's the main thing." Leaning against the damp draining board Una read the *Manchester Guardian* she had bought at Croydon. Makhno's 'insurgent army', consisting predominantly of Ukrainian settlers, Indians, Métis (pushed out of their homelands), and some disaffected Scots and French, had won control of rural Ontario. The main cities, including Ottawa and Toronto, were still in the hands of the R.C.M.P. It was stalemate of

18

sorts, since Makhno's army was defensive and would only respond to attacks, while the Mounties were unwilling to begin any action which would result in bloodshed. Una found this funny: Anarchism matched against Liberalism in a classic dilemma. But London was upset, which was why she had been ordered home from Prague.

The door opened. Catherine hurried in from the landing. ''Oh!'' She was pleased. She wiped rain from her beautiful face and tugged off a headscarf to reveal curly blonde hair. ''How long have you got?''

''I have to be off tomorrow.'' ·

After some hesitation, they embraced.

---

### 3

*The ''Riders of the Plains'', hero-worshipped by readers of wild North-West literature as the ''Mounties'', were formed in 1873 for the purpose of maintaining the law in sparsely populated parts of the Dominion. Recruiting was commenced in 1874, and early in their history their courage and integrity established order and respect in the Indian territory. Although tasks are less picturesque than in the bad old days, diverse activities still include punishment for wrongdoing and the enforcement of Federal Law throughout Canada.*
Soldiers of the King, No. 21, issued by Godfrey Phillips Ltd, c. 1937

---

BY THE TIME Una got there Toronto had capitulated and Makhno's people were everywhere, distributing characteristic anarchist leaflets, informing the citizens of their many rights. Confusingly, numbers of Makhnovischini wore red coats borrowed from disarmed Mounties and a few had even taken the full uniform, though usually with modifications. She went directly to the downtown offices of the Canadian Pacific Airship Company where Major Nye had the responsibility of processing applications from those who had elected to

19

leave. The building was surprisingly quiet, though long lines of middle-aged men and women stood outside it. In the lobby soft-spoken Mounties patiently kept order, manning desks formerly occupied by CPAC clerks. Una was shown straight through to Major Nye's office. It had been decorated in the clean, stripped-pine-and-hessian style favoured by most Canadian executives, while tasteful scenic paintings had been positioned along the walls ˜at regular intervals.

BY THE TIME UNA GOT THERE TOR-
ONTO HAD CAPITULATED AND MAKHNO'S
PEOPLE WERE EVERYWHERE

The large window looked out over Lake Shore Avenue
and the harbour beyond, where other refugees were
crowding onto boats and ships which would take them to
emergency immigration centres at Wilson on the American
side. The United States had agreed reluctantly to establish
temporary camps, but already, Una knew, they were urging
independent Ottawa and Britain to send military ships to
the province, to oust the 'illegal anarchist government', as
they insisted on terming it. Makhno and his insurgents

21

evidently represented the popular interest and since the Mounties had made no attempt to defend the cities by force of arms (on instructions from London, who were anxious to negotiate with Makhno as soon as possible) there was technically no excuse to send either troops or aerial gunboats. The idea of a Commonwealth in which all were free and willing partners had to be maintained, London felt, above everything.

"I mean Britain has always been the guardian of liberal democracy," said Major Nye, after he had offered her a chair and ordered some coffee. "We can't resort to the methods of Frenchmen or Russians, can we? Or even Americans. We've an example to set. There hasn't been a serious clash of arms in the Empire for thirty years. Everything has been settled by discussion, arbitration, common sense. I can't see what they want with anarchism, can you? I mean, the difference seems so marginal!"

"They think," said Una, "of our democracy as capital's last attempt to survive. In, as it were, disguise."

"There'll always be conflicting interests." He remained bewildered. "Besides, there have been socialist governments for years!"

"Makhno's socialism is a trifle more extreme." Una took the coffee cup with a smile of thanks to the girl who came in. "They want me here, I gather, to parley with the Little Father."

"Not many of our people have had much to do with him." Major Nye returned his attention to the lines on the quays. "You know him well, don't you?"

Una came to stand beside him. "We're always looking out of windows, you and I, aren't we?"

He had not heard her. "This is what comes of giving autonomy to Quebec," he said. "Canada simply isn't India."

# 4

DRUMMOND. Motto "Gang warily". Badge, Wild Thyme. The ancestor is said to have been Maurice, a Hungarian, who accompanied Edgar Atheling into Scotland, and obtained from Malcolm III the lands of Drymen. This patriotic clan fought with distinguished bravery at Bannockburn.

Highland Clans, No. 3, issued by John Player and Sons, c. 1920

HALF TORONTO SEEMED deserted now. Named like Ontario's towns and villages for their nostalgic associations with Britain, the quiet streets of the suburbs, with big shady trees and pleasant lawns, were almost wholly taken over by the insurgents to whom the references—Albion Road, Uxbridge Avenue, Ballantrae Drive—were all but meaningless. Certain self-conscious Métis and Indians, who occupied houses on their own farms, had pitched wigwams in the parks and were holding councils with local inhabitants. The smiling residents still found it hard not to be eagerly condescending to those now regarding them with cheerful contempt. The majority of Torontonians remaining behind were the same nationalist sympathisers who had elected the provincial government which had so quickly disappointed their hopes. In reaction, the rural people had made the ageing anarchist their spokesman.

The shirt-sleeved driver of the Rolls landau pointed ahead to a large timber-built house at the end of the road and said in Ukrainian: 'Batko Makhno headquarters. See.'' A black flag had been stuck in a chimney and was visible over the surrounding pines and birches. Una was delighted by the introduction of so much incongruity into this Home Counties dream of Utopia.

Makhno was leaning on the veranda frame as she walked up the crazy-paving towards him. He was greyer and thinner than when she had last seen him during his successful campaigns against the Russian Republic in the thirties, but he had the same alert, sardonic eyes. He wore a jaunty astrakhan cap, a dragoon jacket in blue and gold, civilian jodhpurs and soft Ukrainian boots. Almost as a concession to his past he sported two large automatic pistols and a sabre. Although cured of TB he retained the slight flush often associated with the disease. He burst into laughter as they embraced. "We've done it again. Only this time it was easier!"

"That's what I've come to see you about," said Una.

They entered the cool open-plan interior, full of woollen scatter-rugs of Indian design, polished boards and low furniture in muted colours. A well-fed blonde Canadian girl with a smooth skin which needed to be tanned to look agreeable said brightly: "Hi! I'm Nestor's new wife."

"My twenty-first," said Makhno. He put an arm about her upright shoulders. "This," he said of Una, "is my oldest friend and closest enemy."

"We've heard of you, Miss Persson," said the girl, "even in Toronto."

With a slightly studied display of carelessness, Makhno dropped into a beige armchair near the rough granite fireplace. "Have you come to bargain, Una?"

"In a way. You know you've upset the Americans."

"Certainly. Is that difficult? And the Russians. Our Alaska raid."

"Exactly. Two airships. But London's under a lot of pressure."

"We've already been promised autonomy. The same terms as agreed with Montreal. Everyone is happy."

"The Russians are claiming that by recognising you Canada has violated the Alaskan treaty. Therefore they feel entitled to retaliate. The US would see such a move as the first step in an attempt by Russia to gain further North American territory."

Makhno laughed. "What are you suggesting? Some sort of second Great War?"

"You know there are tensions."

"But no one would risk so much over one tiny event!"

"They see it as the spread of anarchy. First the Ukraine.

24

Then Andalusia. Argentina. Kwan Tung. You know what emotions are involved. Perhaps if you appeared initially to modify your programmes, give them a 'liberal' slant . . .?''

The girl spoke, smiling earnestly, with self-conscious passion, as she tried to persuade Una to a point of view unfamiliar only to herself: ''You have to see, Mrs Persson, that this 'liberalism' is the same sentiment people reserve for the beasts they keep for food. Their love of the masses is love for the lambs they shall one day slaughter! The impulse remains authoritarian, no matter what it pretends to be. Bolsheviks and capitalists. They're identical.''

The phone rang. Makhno went to it. He listened, his smile growing broader as his eyes became sad. He shrugged, replacing the receiver. ''There you are, Mrs Persson. British ships have been sighted over Winnipeg. A large fleet. Evidently on their way here. It's the finish. Obviously. Is it my fault do you think? Have I fallen into the trap I always warned you about? The fallacy of 'history'. The myth of 'precedent'?''

''What shall you do?''

''Oh, I shall avoid bloodshed at all costs. I shall advise the army not to fight in cities, where civilians will be hurt. We shall have to do our fighting in the countryside.'' He sighed. ''Where we belong.''

''But you'll continue to defend the revolution?''

''If people wish it. If not, I'll make a run for it. Not for the first time.''

The pale girl was confused. She squatted on her haunches in the middle of the room, holding her long hair away from her ears. ''Oh, my god. This is *Canada*! We've gone too far!''

Una was much harsher than Makhno. ''Your problem came when the Mounties changed their motto from *Mantien Le Droit* to *Mea virtute me involvo*.''

Makhno interposed. ''If only it could have been *Omnia vincit amor, et nos cedamus amori*.'' He looked regretfully down at the blonde. ''It'll be good to be on horseback again. I hate machines.''

"It's your one weakness, I'm afraid," said Una.
The silence became uncertain.

---

## 5

### CORONATION OF WILLIAM IV AND QUEEN ADELAIDE.

*The Coronation of William IV took place on Sept. 8th, 1831, and was celebrated with less magnificence than usual on the ground of economy. The Queen's silver crown was set with jewels which were her own property, and were afterwards returned to her, as she desired that there should be no unnecessary expense incurred.*
The Coronation Series, No. 31, issued by W.D. & H.O. Wills, c. 1936

---

THERE WAS, IT seemed, to be no consolation in England. Over tea in Derry and Toms roof garden ('their' place) Catherine told Una of her engagement to Mr Koutrouboussis, the ship-owner. "His naturalisation came through last week and he popped the question."

"You don't love him." Una was bleak.

"I love what he represents."

"Slavery!"

"Freedom. I shan't be his only interest."

The sun shone on large mock-silver cutlery, on sturdy china, on rock-cakes and scones. Beyond all this, in tiny artificial pools, marched fastidious pink flamingos against a background of box and privet.

"And anyway," Catherine continued, "I need the security."

"I'm giving up the Service."

"I think you should." She realised she had missed the implication and melted. "You know how much I love you."

"Going back into the profession," Una said.

26

Catherine put a hand on Una's hand. "You'd still be away a lot, dear. But now we can go on meeting—having lovely secret times. You already have more men-friends than I do. That anarchist was one, wasn't he?"

It was true. Una removed her hand in order to open her bag.

"I really do think men are our superiors in almost every way," said Catherine. She smiled. "Of course, we are their superiors in one area—we can handle them without them realising it. But don't you feel the need to give yourself up to a man? To think you could die for him, if necessary? Oh, Una, there's nothing like self-sacrifice!"

"Jesus Christ," said Una flatly. "He's done it again."

## 6

*MEADOW BROWN (Epinephele ianira). This species is the most abundant of all British Butterflies, occurring throughout the British Islands as far north as the Orkneys, and frequenting every meadow, lane, wood and waste land, from the middle of June until the middle of October. The Meadow Brown is one of the few butterflies that appear regardless of the weather, flying during dull stormy days, as well as in the hottest sunshine. At night it roosts amongst the foliage of trees, and also on low-growing plants. The life of the caterpillar of this butterfly extends over a period of about 250 days. Expanse of wings 2 inches.*

British Butterflies, No. 15, issued by W.D. & H.O. Wills, c. 1935

EXACTLY A WEEK after she had had her meeting with Makhno, on Sunday 27th June 1948, Una Persson accepted Major Nye's invitation. She took a train to Rye and a cab from the station to the Jacobean house whose ornamental gardens had been almost entirely converted into fruit and vegetable beds and whose stables were now run as a commercial enterprise by Elizabeth Nye, one of the major's two daughters. His son was away at school. His wife had been confined to her rooms for three or four years.

It was a very hot day. Summer flowers, arranged in dense clusters and grown for profit, gave off a thick scent which brought Una a trace of euphoria as well as sad memories of Makhno's fall. The nurse who looked after Mrs Nye directed Una to the stables. Elizabeth had taken a group of children for a trek. Major Nye, in a worn tweed hacking jacket, darned pullover, moleskin trousers and old wellingtons, stood outside a stall over which the name 'Rhodes' had been engraved in poker-work. He was feeding an ancient grey horse handfuls of grass from a bucket at his feet. The horse had watering, bloodshot eyes and its nostrils were encrusted with mucus. It laid its ears back as Una approached, causing Major Nye to turn.

"Mrs Persson! Wonderful! This is Rhodes." The smell

from the stall was strong, tinged with sickness.

Una, who had no special fondness for horses, stretched a hand to stroke its nose but it moved, refusing contact. "I'm afraid he's a one-man horse. I'm so glad the Canadian business is over. Have you heard anything of our friend, Makhno?"

Rather closer to self-pity than she would have liked, Una said: "He's gone where the Southern cross the Yellow Dog."

"Eh?"

"On his way to South America, I heard."

"Best place for him. Plenty of room for political experiments there, eh?"

"Not according to everyone's thinking."

"At least we avoided a Big One. You see I remember the Great War. I was at Geneva in 1910. Eighteen years old." He smiled and patted Rhodes's nose. "We don't want another, do we?"

"Perhaps the cost of peace has become a bit too high?"

"It's never too high, my dear. I speak as an army man." He handed her the bucket. "Rhodes can't graze for himself any more. Shaky on his pins. Come and help me pick some grass on that bit of lawn over there." He reached down to pluck a muddy *Telegraph* from a pile near the stall's gate. "Kneel on this. Have you got any older clothes?"

"Not with me."

"We'll find you something. You're staying a week or two?"

"If that's all right."

"All right for me." He chuckled. She realised that she had never seen him happy before. "They've allowed you some leave, have they? You've earned it. Makhno would never had given in to anyone else."

"Possibly." Una was reluctant to continue this line. "But I'm not on holiday. I've resigned. I've decided to go back to the stage. I'm tired of diplomacy. It's a bit depressing. Or perhaps I'll try films."

"Brave girl," said Major Nye. "You've sacrificed too much already."

For a moment she rebelled, resenting his approval. Then she walked over to a lawn already practically bare, and began to tug up grass.

Major Nye joined her. He bent with difficulty. There was a tearing sound as he pulled roots and earth. "They all say I should have him shot. But I can't do it, you know. I love him. Elizabeth," he smiled with some pride, "says he'll be the death of me."

The shadow of an airship, going from Croydon to the continent, passed over them rapidly. They heard the distant drone of engines.

"It's the beginning of the end," murmured Major Nye.

"It always is," said Una.

# DEVELOPMENT (a)

## Pierrot on the Moon

They didn't tell me
That breathing was so difficult.
I can't say I think
much
Of the scenery
I wish I was back
in my home again
—They've left me behind . . .

It seemed a good
idea at the time
Just me—Harlequin and
Columbine
—But they slipped off soon
And here I am
Stranded on the bloody
moon . . .

Next time things will be
different
And I'll know the score
I'll bring at least an
oxygen tent
And a good deal more
besides
Bacon, eggs and bread
And a telescope . . .

And I'll buy returns as well
There's no bloody ticket office
Or a gentleman's lavatory
Or a deck chair to be had
And every time I take a step—
I bounce . . .

They said it'd be just like
Brighton beach
Dodgems and roundabouts
Candy floss and sticks of rock
Though not so many crowds
Try and get a donkey ride
That's all I've got to say . . .


## Harlequin's Techniques of Courtship

If I let her see my love
Will she also see my pain
And flee from it
As I would flee?

And if I pulled my domino
From my eyes
Would she then know
How much of Pierrot's
Left in Harlequin?

And if I told her of my yearning
Would her body
Cease to burn for me
Instead would she give me
Only sympathy
And mistress turn to wife?

And if I swore eternal love
In anything but
A tone of insincerity
Would I alert her
To involvement
Turn her thoughts
Away from lust?

And if I wept upon her breast
And spoke of fears
Of ghosts and death
Would she withdraw
Her favours from me
Choosing silly Pierrot
For a husband
And shunning me?

No, I can only speak of bright lies
Offer only flattery
Tell her that there are no others
But let her think that many follow
That I may be gone tomorrow
Insecurity is all she wants
From me.
Madam, I present myself:
Sir Harlequin—
I bring you Sin . . .

## Columbine Confused

On the banks of Time's river
Two lovers await me
As the flood takes me by
They reach out their hands
Pierrot and Harlequin
Weeping they greet me
The stream bears me onward
Future and Past . . .

Which shall I choose?
Oh, I am confused . . .
Often amused and
Constantly torn . . .
Down the long centuries
They have pursued me
Courted and cursed me
For what I am

Gravity holds me
In sweet indecision
Between Sun and Moon
To each I'm attracted
Pierrot and Harlequin
Loser and Trickster
Laughing they beckon
As the years flood away

Future and past
Future and past
Future and past
Future and past

As the years flood away
As the years flood away
As they years flood away
Future and past . . .

# 2. THE KASSAND — RA PENINSULA

*In which his torment often was so great,*
  *That like a Lyon he would cry and rore,*
  *And rend his flesh, and his owne synewes eat.*
  *His owne deare Vna hearing euermore*
  *His ruefull shriekes and gronings, often tore*
  *Her guiltless garments, and her golden heare,*
  *For pitty of his paine and anguish sore;*
    *Yet all with patience wisely she did beare;*
*For well she wist, his crime could else be neuer cleare.*

Spenser, The Fairie Queene, 1. x. 28.

UNA CONSIDERED HER compact. It was silver, with delicate enamel-work by Brule; one of his last pieces.

"Una."

She shook her head. She refused his confession. His eyes were agony.

"Una."

She replaced the compact, unused, in her patent leather purse. His voice brought her the image of a dark, motionless sea. She drew breath. Makhno had gone on. It had been necessary. His success—what little he expected—depended on the speed of his strategies. Here there was only defeat.

"Una."

He lay in the shadows, on straw. Through the barn door came the hard air of the New Hampshire winter. She could see across the deep, undulating snow the flat outline of a Dutch farmhouse, black against a near-white sky: the isolated birches, the clustering pines. She could hear the muffled sounds of work. It would be dawn in a moment. They would discover him soon. Freezing her face, Una forced herself to look at her ex-comrade. He had seemed so powerful.

"Una." It was like the sound of a dying albatross she had heard on Midway Island in the early 1940s.

One of his hands moved a fraction. To stop her? To beg?

She glanced beyond his head, at the disused harness, the rusty implements: mementos of simpler days. She smoothed the silk of her skirt and swung the purse by its strap; then she placed it carefully on her shoulder. She battled against her particular curse, against mindless altruism. But was it a curse or merely her permanent dilemma?

"Una. They'll kill me."

"No, Jerry." He would probably be interned until after the primaries. She was close to offering reassurance when happily there came a scream from the sky and snow thudded from the roof of the barn as a pirate Concorde passed overhead, pursued by angry Freedom Fighters. It was so cold and she, like him, had no appropriate clothing. "Montreal." she said. "Try to get to Montreal. I'll see you there." She stepped in black, high-heeled court-shoes into the snow. She shuddered. It had been stupid of them to trust the old Kamov.

## 2

*'I'm ready when you are, Senor . . .'*

Bob Dylan

"WE BEGIN WITH ambiguities and then we strive to reconcile them through the logic of Art," said Prinz Lobkowitz. "Though these chaps often begin with some simple idea and then try to achieve ambiguity through obfuscation. It won't do." He threw the composition paper on the floor beside the piano and got up. "I blame the academics."

Something rumbled underfoot.

"Well," she said, "it's easy."

She leaned back on the piano stool and swung round to peer at the half-built auditorium. She could see the night sky through the gaps in the tarpaulins covering the shattered glass of the dome; another publicist's broken dream. Lobkowitz, in evening dress, loped forward, tall and thin, looking less well than usual. His attempt, at the invitation of the United States provisional government, to form a cabinet had failed, as he had predicted it would. As a result both he and Una were out of their jobs. She was relieved; he was contemplative. The meeting, which had been held earlier that evening, in the light of candles and oil-lamps, had taken on the air of a funeral reception. Then, gradually, the distinguished old men had drifted away. All but a few of the lamps were out. It was a shame that the damp had affected the murals, from Mozart to Messiaen, on the hastily emulsioned walls. She appreciated the peculiarities of Gregg's style, with its muted colours and shadowy outlines. She had particularly liked the portrait of Schoenberg, on stage for *Pierrot Lunaire* in Berlin, 1912. Now, however, only the composer's raised hands were perceivable, as if he conducted the invisible crowd, here muting the antagonistic shouts, there bringing up the applause. Una wished she could explain her sudden feeling of well-being. She swung to smile at Lobkowitz who shrugged, grinning back at her.

"Ah, well."

"We search so hard for these intense experiences. Then we reject them almost at once."

"Is it because we are frightened?"

## 3

*'There are jewels in the crown of England's Glory;*
   *And every jewel shines a thousand ways*
*Frankie Howerd and Noel Coward and Garden Gnomes*
   *Frankie Vaughan and Kenneth Horne and Sherlock Holmes*
*Monty and Biggles and Old King Cole, in the pink or on the dole*
   *Oliver Twist and Long John Silver, Captain Cook and*
   *Nellie Dean*
*Enid Blyton, Gilbert Harding, Malcolm Sargeant, Graham Greene*
*Gra-ham Gree--ne!'*

Max Wall

RELUCTANTLY SHE PICKED up the Ak-47 as Petrov pushed pouches of ammunition across the table at her.

"It suits you," he said. "It's elegant, isn't it?" He lit a thin Danemann cheroot. "You know the rifle?"

"Oh, yes." She checked its action. "I was hoping I'd never see one again." The smoke from his cheroot made her feel sick.

"There's the M-60 . . ." He made a movement towards the rack.

"No, no." She clipped the pouches to the webbing of her lightweight camouflage jacket. She wished that she did not feel quite so comfortable in the gear. It was suspicious. Another cloud of smoke reached her face. She turned away.

"You have everything else?" he asked. "Plenty of mosquito oil?"

"Plenty. Can't you tell?" She wiped her fingers over the back of her greasy wrist.

He stood up.

"Una."

"Oh, no you don't," she said. Helping the wounded was no longer any part of her brief.

"It's you I'm thinking of." He sat down again, staring beyond her at the veldt on the other side of the border. He brightened, pointing. "Look. Vultures."

She did not turn.

He was grinning. "They're a protected species now!"

Carefully she closed the screen door behind her and stood on the veranda, looking up the road for her transport. It was already half-an-hour late. She wondered if something had happened to it. If so, it would mean a long wait while they radioed back to Kinshasa for instructions. She glanced at her watch without reading it. She had never been over-fond of Africa. Somehow, in spite of everything, they had continued to look to Europe for their models. Just like the Americans. And here she was, Britannia Encyclopaedia, returned for the shoot-out.

"You 'ave ter larf, don't yer, miss?" said the black

cockney corporal, holding up the water-can in which
someone had shot two small holes. His heavy boots made
the veranda shake as he went by, entering Petrov's office to
request an order.

She sat down in a khaki deck-chair, placing the rifle at
her feet. She stretched her body. The corporal came out
again. "Seen anything o' that Captain Cornelius, miss?"
he asked, to pass the time. "'E was 'ere before the real
trouble started."

She laughed.

"He usually is."

" THAT CAPTAIN CORNELIUS, MISS, 'E WAS 'ERE BEFORE THE REAL TROUBLE STARTED. "

## 4

*In the event of a Sonic Attack, follow these rules:*

Hawkwind

AS THE RIVER broadened, she became alert, releasing the safety catch, crouching in the front of the motor launch and studying the jungle.

She gave particular attention to the thicker clumps of reeds on both banks. Soon she had made out the funnels and the bridge of an old steamer which had been ambushed here two years before. *The Little Madam* had keeled over so that she was almost on her side; she was rusty and plants clung to her. As Una watched, a small crocodile emerged from one of the funnels and wriggled into the water. *The Little Madam* had been the last of her kind. She had been carrying missionaries back to the coast when a handful of Eritreans, lost and on the run, had mistaken her for a military vessel and used the rest of their mortars on her.

There was a horrible silence in the jungle, as if every bird and insect had been blown away. Yet the foliage itself was lusher than ever; fleshy and dark green. They approached a bend. A huge stretch of dirty detergent scum came swirling towards them and passed on both sides of the labouring launch.

In the stern Shakey Mo Collier, watched by a listless Makhno who had drunk at least twenty cans of local beer, was jumping up and down throwing carved wooden idols into the scum. "Fuck you! Fuck you!" He drew the idols from a bulky sack, almost as large as himself. He had been upset to learn that his loot had become valueless since the falling off of the tourist trade.

The jungle on the right bank ended suddenly, to be replaced by the great grey terraced complex of Durango Industries' protein processing plant. Una tried not to breath any of the sweet air until they were past. Nearby were the white buildings of the hospital, identified by their red crosses, looking remarkably like reception buildings for the plant. It could have been one of the sleazier suburbs of Los Angeles, with huge, unhealthy palm trees growing all around. Workers on the roofs and gantries paused to watch the launch. Collier waved at them but lost interest when nobody waved back.

"Surly buggers." He threw the last of his idols in their direction.

Makhno was asleep. Una was relieved. If he slept, there was not so much danger of his being sick over the seats. They were already slimy with a variety of filth.

Mo moved along the boat to stand beside her. He lit a papyruska lifted from the tunic pocket of some fallen foe. "There won't be trouble here, will there?"

"Unlikely." She wiped her forehead. "The worst is over. It seems we'll be slipping this shipment through, at least."

"I'm making bloody sure I get my bonus in my hand next time." Mo scowled. "In gold." He patted his belt pouch. It bulged. From under the tightly-buttoned flap a few fair hairs emerged.

Una still marvelled at Mo's ability to adopt enthusiastically the ideals and ambitions of any employer. A day or so earlier she had asked him about this. He had replied: "I enjoy being loyal."

He had earned his high reputation. He had even earned his Russian scalps (he would pass them off, of course, as Rhodesian).

For all his awful habits, Una enjoyed his company and she would be sorry to part, but with the successful delivery of their cargo her mission would be over. She was glad the journey had been relatively swift. No amount of disinfectant or perfume could disguise the smell from the hold. It was the last time, she promised herself, that she took over one of Cornelius's jobs. He had only taken this one on so as not to lose face, to protect a reputation for ruthlessness which he had never really deserved.

Collier could continue with the load to Dubrovnik and get a plane home from there if he wanted to. But she would take her chances at the ports. She had had enough.

## 5

*'Isn't it delicious? There's a red sun in the sky! Every time we see it rise, another city dies . . .'*

The Deep Fix

"OF COURSE, I remember him from the early, carefree days," said Miss Brunner, smiling up at the crystal ball which turned in the centre of the ceiling of Lionel Himmler's Blue Spot Club. "He was much better company, then." She seemed to imply that that had been before he had met Una. There was nothing superficially attractive about the woman, in her severe suit; her awkward, almost self-conscious way of moving; but Una experienced a strong desire to make love to her, perhaps because she sensed no hint of resonance, no sympathy for Miss Brunner. She tried to suppress the desire; she had a good idea of any consequences resulting from even a brief affair. "When he was still idealistic," continued Miss Brunner. "Weren't we all?"

"I still am," said Una. "It's silly isn't it?" She was shocked at herself. That last remark was unlike her. She admired Miss Brunner's power to produce it.

47

Miss Brunner gave her a smile which might have been of sympathy or of triumph. "When you're as old a campaigner as me, dear, you won't have time for that sort of thing." She signed to the sour-faced Jewish waiter. As he approached, she pressed a coin in his hand. "Bartok's String Quartet No. 1," she said. She watched him shuffle towards the juke-box. It was her turn to display embarrassment. "I'm feeling a bit reflective. You weren't about in the old days, of course."

"It depends what you mean," said Una.

"Our paths hadn't crossed, at any rate."

"No." Una wondered how, with so many wounds, the woman could continue to function.

Miss Brunner sipped her B&B. From the fur collar of her jacket came the smell of artificial hyacinths. "It's nice to know someone's prepared to fill in for him."

"I'm not exactly filling in," said Una. "I think you have the wrong impression."

"That's what they told me at the Time Centre."

"Auchinek?"

"No, the other one. Alvarez."

"He only enjoyed working with Cornelius."

"That's true."

"Of course you move about more than any of us ever did, don't you?" Miss Brunner continued.

"I suppose I do."

"I envy you your freedom. I'm afraid I'm very old fashioned."

Una was amused by the series of ploys. "Oh, no," she said.

"A terrible reactionary, eh?"

"Not at all."

"I came out of a very different school." Reminiscently Miss Brunner smacked her lips.

"It's just a question of temperaments," said Una.

"Well we each of us see what we're looking for. Especially in a man. That's what 'knowing' someone means, doesn't it?"

48

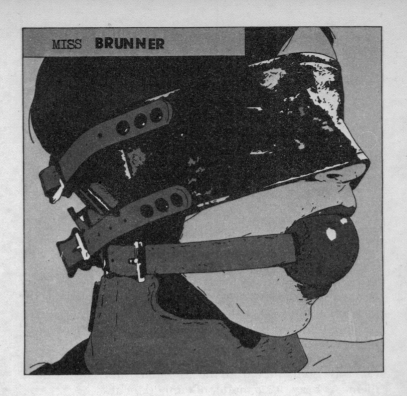

The waiter returned, just as the scratched record began to play.

"I hate Bartok." Miss Brunner picked up the menu. "I find him empty. Vivaldi's what I really like, but the selection's so limited here." She peered savagely up at the waiter. "I'll have the *moules* to begin."

"They're Danish," said the waiter.

"That's right. And then the jugged hare."

"Just an omelette." Una made no attempt to read the menu in the dim light. "And some mineral water."

"Plain omelette? Perrier?"

"Fine."

"Anyway," said Miss Brunner as she handed the menu

49

to the waiter, "Collier got through with that last consignment. Which about wraps Africa *and* South America up."

"It's a relief."

"It must be for you. I'll be going back to Sweden tomorrow. It's where I live now."

"Yes."

"You know Sweden?"

"Oh, yes."

"Kiruna?"

"Yes."

"It's so peaceful."

Una could not bring herself to confirm any of these desperate affirmations. As a result Miss Brunner became agitated and cast about for another weapon.

"He was never straightforward," she said at length. "That's what I couldn't stand."

"Well, some of us need to create an atmosphere of ambiguity in which we can thrive." Una hoped the response wasn't too evidently direct.

"I don't quite follow you, dear." Miss Brunner had understood all too readily.

Una dispensed with caution. "While others of course try to resolve something from the ambiguity they sense around them. As I say, it's a matter of temperament."

"It's obvious which kind of temperament meets with your approval."

Una smiled. "Yes."

"Speaking for myself, all I want is a quiet life. You didn't get that with Cornelius. He'd foul anything up."

"I probably didn't know him as well as you did."

"Very few people could have done."

Miss Brunner's mussels arrived. She bent her angry head over the bowl.

# 6

*'Their snakeskin suits packed with Detroit muscle . . .'*
Bruce Springsteen

IT WAS A relief to enter the car and stuff Ives's First Symphony into the player. It wasn't that she had objected to the Bartok, but Himmler's ancient recordings, always too heavy on the bass and worn and scratched, made everything sound awful. Of course Himmler regarded even this as a concession. When he had opened the nightclub there had been nothing but Phoenix records to play—a label devoted entirely to Hitler's speeches and National Socialist songs. It had been founded by Arnold Leese, best remembered for calling Mosely a 'Kosher Fascist'. This description was more appropriate to Himmler himself who had, in 1944, changed his name from Gutzmann. It was amazing, she thought, as the music began, how she was warming to America since it had rejected her.

She drove through a cleaned-out Soho, her body filled with sound from the quad speakers in the AMC Rambler Station Wagon she currently favoured. She had never been happy with non-automatics, and though this car had seen more exciting days it provided a secure environment in a world which, at present, she preferred for its chaos. The alternatives to chaos were all too suspect. With the volume as high as possible it was impossible to hear either the engine, the air-conditioning or the few other noises from the streets. This and her sound-proofed flat helped her keep herself to herself. Just now, she had no time for civilians or casualties. The abandoned strip-joints and casinos behind her, she made for Hyde Park as the second movement began. It was hard to believe that this was the conception of a seventeen-year-old. She yearned for her lost youth.

Studying her hands as they rested casually on the large steering wheel she almost crashed into the pack of dogs crossing the road in front of her. The dogs were the reason why it was now only safe to drive through the park.

Mongrels, greyhounds, alsatians, chows and poodles ran erratically, snapping at one another's necks and flanks, and disappeared into the shrubs. She turned out of the park into Bayswater Road, passed Notting Hill Gate and the ruins of the apartment buildings blocking Kensington Park Road, made a right into Ladbroke Grove then, eventually, another right into Blenheim Crescent, stopping outside the seedy terraced house she feared so much, even though it sheltered at least one of the people she loved.

She disembarked from the car and locked it carefully, putting the keys into the pocket of her long black trench-coat. She turned up her collar, mounted the cracked steps, found the appropriate bell and pressed it. She leaned on the door, watching the Co-op milkman as his van moved slowly down the other side of the street making deliveries. Una pressed the bell again, knowing that there was bound to be someone up. It was almost seven o'clock. There was no reply. The milkman came back along the other side of the road. Una pressed the bell for the third time. The milkman climbed the steps with five pints in his arms. He set them at her feet. "You're up early," he said. "Who you after?"

"Cornelius," she said.

He laughed, shaking his head as he went away.

Una found his attitude irritatingly mysterious and would have followed him to question him had not she heard a cautious movement on the other side of the door. She stepped out of view, huddling against the broken pillar of the porch. The door rattled. It opened a fraction. A red hand reached for the milk.

"Good morning," said Una.

The hand withdrew, but the door did not shut.

"Mrs Cornelius?"

"Not in," said an unmistakable voice. "Bugger orf."

"It's Una Persson."

The door opened wider and Mrs Cornelius stood there, in curlers, her woolly dressing gown drawn about her, her bleary eyes blinking. "Ha!" she said. "Thort you woz ther

MRS. CORNELIUS.

bleedin' milkman." Now Una knew why he had laughed.
It was why there had been no answer to the bell—the
combination of bottles rattling and the doorbell ringing
sent Mrs Cornelius automatically to cover. "Wotcha
want?"

"Actually I was looking for Catherine."

"Actcherly, she ain't 'ere."

Mrs Cornelius relented. "Orl right, luv, come in." She
took two pints from the step, darted a look along the street,
admitted Una, closed the door.

Una followed Mrs Cornelius, ascending stone stairs still
bearing traces of broken linoleum; they reached a landing
and a half-open door. She entered a room full of
unattractive smells—cabbage, lavender water, beer,

cigarette smoke. It was immediately evident that Catherine had been here recently, for the flat was tidier than usual. The piles of old weeklies were stacked neatly beside the sideboard which, though cluttered with Mrs Cornelius's cryptic souvenirs, lacked the bottles, cans and empty packages she allowed to accumulate while her daughter was not in residence. Mrs Cornelius made for the gas-stove in the far corner, picked up the dented kettle and filled it at the tap over the sink. Una could see through to Mrs Cornelius's small, dark bedroom, with its huge wardrobe, its walls covered with photographs, many of them cut from magazines and newspapers. The other door was shut. This was the door to Catherine's room.

"She's not up yet, lazy bitch," said Mrs Cornelius. "Cuppa tea?" She relaxed and was friendly. Of her children's acquaintances Una was one of the few Mrs Cornelius actually liked. It did not stop Una being afraid of the woman as of nobody else.

"Thanks." Una hated the prospect.

Mrs Cornelius shuffled to her daughter's door and hammered on it. "Wakey, wakey, rise an' shine. 'Ere's yer mate fer yer!"

"What?" It was Catherine.

Mrs Cornelius laughed. "It'd take the 'Orn o' Fate ter get 'er up!"

Suddenly the whole flat smelled of rose water. It was wonderful; a miracle.

"Bugger," said Mrs Cornelius, picking up the fallen bottle.

---

## 7

*'In the heart of the city, where the alligators roam, I'm a little lost lamb. Ain't got no place to go . . .'*

Nick Lowe

---

SHE FOUND LOBKOWITZ where she had last met him, in the ruined auditorium. Through the speakers of an inefficient tannoy came the familiar last passages of the *Browning Overture*. Then there was silence.

"Browning was a prose Wagner and so was Ives," said the Prinz as he dusted down his tweed fishing suit.

"You've been seeing Cornelius. Is he back?"

"With a vengeance. Though not a very big one."

"Anything I'd recognise."

"You know his penchants . . ."

"I'm not surprised, though I felt he'd crack."

Prinz Lobkowitz seemed to tire of this exchange. He leaned against the warped piano. "There's rarely any danger of that. He just goes dormant."

"I was right to trust my instincts, then?"

"Always, Una."

"They're so hard to rationalise."

"We waste too much time, trying to produce quick resolutions, when usually they're on the way and we don't know it."

She was amused. "The voice of experience!"

"I hope so."

"Anyway, he's better?"

"Yes, he's better. The usual fever. We all suffer from that."

She was not sure this was true of her, but she said: "I was never any good at instant decisions."

"Maybe because you had more to lose than anybody else."

She shrugged.

"Anyway," he continued wistfully, "you received his message?"

"It was unmistakable."

"You didn't have to fulfil all his obligations. He was grateful when he heard."

"There were other people involved. It wasn't his ego I was worried about. He was stupid to have tried for the Presidency. Then, of all times! He was never what you'd call a convinced republican, or a democrat, in the accepted sense."

«ACUTE DEPRESSION OFTEN FOLLOWS A PERIOD OF FRENETIC ACTIVITY.»

"Surely, though, that's why he tried?"

She nodded. "I'm glad America's pulled a couple of decent chestnuts out of the fire."

"You couldn't say they deserved it. But I'm sentimental about George Washington, too. Chile, Brazil, the Argentine—their worst crime was a kind of naïve complacency. Admittedly that attitude leads to excesses of brutality in the long run." Lobkowitz yawned. "I've never seen so much jungle on fire. And whole mountains. The

apocalypse. I wish you'd been here.''

"I had to go back to England.''

"I know.'' He was sympathetic. He put a white hand on her shoulder. "Will you stay for a while now? In New England? You have a place in the Appalachians, haven't you?''

"A couple, at different ends. But there's a sub-tenant in one. He must have been there forty years or more. It would be interesting to see how he's getting on. I haven't aged that much. Not superficially.''

He shook his head. "You can be very vague at times. Feminine, eh?''

"Is that what it is?" She bent to kiss his hand. "Have you got the map? I'd better be going.''

## 8

"YOU'RE STILL LOOKING ill." She tried to disguise any hint of sympathy. She forced her mouth into disapproving lines.

"They don't treat you very well. But I'm grateful, really. It kept me out of the war. I always wondered how I'd do it.''

"You thought you could stop it. You remember?''

He was bashful. "Oh, yes. So thanks again.''

All his old charm had returned and it was hard for her not to warm to him, as she had first warmed, long ago. The self-pity was gone, for the moment, and he had a good deal of his old style. He fingered the collar of his black car coat, turning the lapels so that they framed his pale face. "It's cold for spring.''

"The long range forecasts are predicting an Ice Age again.''

"Always a bad psychological sign. And the computers?''

"That we'll all be dead in a year or two.''

He grinned. "Acute depression often follows a period of frenetic activity. You'll see—in a few months the weather forecasts will give us brilliant summers, plenty of rain for the crops, mild winters, and the computers will be going on about a Golden Age." He put his arm around her shoulders. It was awful how quickly her resolutions disappeared. Her struggle lasted less than a second. "Stick with me, baby," he promised, "and it will always be a golden age somewhere.''

"That's not what you were saying the last time we spoke," she reminded him.

"We all suffer from depression occasionally." He dismissed the creature he had been. Probably he didn't remember. She began to think that his attitude was the healthiest.

She climbed into the driving seat of the Rambler. He sat beside her, watching her with approval as she started the big car. "It's a good thing petrol's cheap again. Where are we going? Concord?"

"Yes. First." As she started the engine the tape she had been playing came on. He reached to remove it. "Enough of that classical stuff," he said. "Let's have something romantic and jolly." He sorted through the box of cartridges on the seat between them. "Here we are."

He slotted the *Holiday Symphony* into the player. "Much better."

He leaned back in the car as she drove it down the bumpy track to the empty highway.

"That's what I like about you, Una. You know how to relax."

# DEVELOPMENT (b)

## Pierrot's Song
## of Positive Thinking

I'm glad I'm not dead
I'm glad I'm not dead
I'm glad I'm not dead
I'm glad I'm not dead
I'm glad I'm not dead
I'm glad I'm not dead
I'm glad I'm not dead
I'm glad I'm not


## The Nature of the Catastrophe

Can anyone suggest an explanation
Can anyone please suggest an explanation
Can anyone suggest an explanation


## Through the Megaflow (Waltz)

Oh, Columbine
I'm lost in Time,
There ain't a sign
Of ho-o-ome . . .

Where is—where is—
My lovely Columbine?

She took a trip
On an old time ship
There was a slip
And now she's lost
Alone . . .

She could be
In Nine O Three
Or Twenty Million and Six
She told me
That she'd be free
But now she's lost her fix . . .

Oh, Columbine
Sweet love of mine
I missed you so
On the megaflow

Where is—where is—
My lovely Columbine?

She said we'd meet
In a place so neat
Say June of Fifty Seven,
But catastrophe
She could not beat
So maybe she's in Heaven . . .

Where is—where is—
My lovely Columbine?
Where is—where is—
My lovely Columbine?

# 3. REVOLUTIONS

# 1

## GET CRACKING ON KELLOGG'S

*Barnie stacks bricks as quick as some people talk, and he never drops them. 'Course it's simply a case of cause and effect. You see, his Missus knows that at least a quarter of a man's daily output of energy must come from his 8 o'clock intake of calories\*. So she gives him Kellogg's Corn Flakes for energy and warmth. Food needn't be hot to warm you. Human beings take their fuel from energy-giving foods (chiefly carbohydrates) that are burned up in the body. Kellogg's are extremely rich in carbohydrates—so they give you energy and keep you warm.*

*\*Calories are units of heat that measure the amount of energy different foods provide.*

ADVERTISEMENT: Picture Post, 1 March 1952

---

"THOSE POOR DEVILS," said Colonel Pyat, "they cannot survive in the world of the imagination. They are afraid of it. They reject it as vulgar, or over-coloured or—what? And then they offer us their threadbare language, their worn-out images as—" he sniggered "—poetry."

"If I were you, colonel, I would be concentrating on the immediate problems." Nestor Makhno shifted his weight as best he could. At least the truck was moving fairly rhythmically now and the swaying could be anticipated. They must be on one of the pieces of autobahn which had been extended into Bohemia in the days before the war. The men were tied to each wheel of a huge, old-fashioned 120mm field-gun. "I'm not impressed by your sudden discovery of the romantic agony."

"Particularly since it was our money which helped you make it." In the corner, near the only place where the canopy was loose enough to let in a breeze and the occasional light from a passing vehicle's headlamps, Una Persson looked up from the rope which bound her hands. She had been trying to gnaw it but her mouth kept growing intolerably dry. She referred to the cocaine Colonel Pyat had bought with cash set aside for bribing their way out of

COLONEL PYAT HAD ADDRESSED THE SOLDIERS AS COMRADES AND TRIED TO APPEAL TO THEIR SENSE OF LIBERTY ...

Bohemia. At Passau, on the Danube, they had been changing trains with the other passengers when several militia-men had stopped them. At that time Colonel Pyat had been even more euphoric than now. He had addressed the soldiers as comrades and tried to appeal to their sense of liberty. Consequently he and the others had been searched and their weapons discovered. Now they were on their way back to Prague. Una knew that there was every possibility of treating with the new authorities and getting free again, but she was worried in case someone should link her name with that of Lobkowitz, who would be arriving on *The Kansas City Whirlwind* the next day, brought back, once more, from exile in America. Lobkowitz's peculiar mixture of anarcho-syndicalism and despotism had an appeal to all the factions involved in the Slavic Border Wars. Everyone was tired of the present cant, all of which denied authoritarianism and displayed it in every action. With a bit of luck the Czechs and Slovaks and Poles and Galiceans and Bylorussians and the rest would see some virtue in the example of Ukrainia, whose anarchism had given the country stability, relative wealth and security from outside attack, and had since Istanbul had been razed by the so-called suicide fleet of Cypriot airships five years before, turned Kiev and Odessa into the most vital cultural centres of Europe or the Middle East. She turned her face against the cold stream of air and wet her lips. She was half-way through the rope and congratulated her captors for their contempt of her femininity when they had casually tied her hands in front of her. Makhno and Pyat were much more secure. If she used all her strength now, she might even snap the rope. But she continued to chew. In the meantime Nestor Makhno was rubbing fruitlessly, trying to find a suitably sharp place on the field-gun, while Colonel Pyat's voice rose higher and higher as he elaborated his indignation, expressing cosmic disgust at their plight, offering cosmic solutions, the broadest of comforts.

Una sympathised with him. The tight, worried, stupid faces of the local authorities, who had sneered at them and sent them back to Prague, were still in her mind. There was nothing more depressing than those faces: men and women who, through expediency and fear, served a revolutionary cause they could not understand. She had seen so many of them. They continued to depress her. For some reason there were always more of them around railway stations than anywhere else. Perhaps the tracks and the timetables offered less ambiguity than the rest of the world. Wristwatches were important to them, too, she remembered. And tightly-buckled coats. It was interesting to note how in the early, wild and enthusiastic days of the Revolution the characteristic costume was a great-coat flung open, a hat askew, a hand spread outwards; later the representations of leaders became identified with neatly-buttoned uniforms, well-set caps and firm salutes, and only the Cossacks, as in Tsarist times, had been allowed to display a certain 'freedom', to represent the glories of irresponsibility. The new Tsars, in Muscovia, favoured the casual-bourgeois style of middle-aged German business-men on holiday: cashmere pullovers, well-creased grey slacks, plaid sports-jackets and straight-stemmed briar pipes. It was what they felt, Una assumed, the people wanted—middle-class monarchy, armchair imperialism. She feared those people almost as much as she feared the police-caste Pyat still raved against.

"They destroy so much in the name of safety. They destroy those who have enabled their kind to survive for millenia. Without us, they would die out!" Pyat continued.

Makhno was amused. "Us? Your Zaporozhian Cossacks were not the most liberal and pacific of people."

"The Cossacks held liberty to be their most prized possession!" Pyat had long-since revealed, by his mistakes, that he had no Cossack background at all, but had been born in the slums of Minsk, probably of half-Jewish parents. He had fled Ukrainia in the uniform of a Zaporozhian Cossack colonel and for a while had benefited from the deception. But Makhno enjoyed pretending to believe the lie.

"And were prepared to kill every Jewish baby to defend their liberty!" The anarchist laughed.

"Don't blame the Cossacks for that!" said Pyat with heat. "It was all the fault of the Polish landlords who leased their Russian lands to Jews. A lot of Jews said so themselves."

"You mean the Jews blamed the Poles for letting them bleed Ukrainians?" Makhno flexed his arms. "My God!"

"You're as anti-semitic as the rest of them." Pyat spoke in that peculiar, detached tone he always affected when the subject of Jews was raised. He thought the tone lofty. Sometimes it deceived and angered a less perceptive hearer. But it aroused Makhno's sympathy. The

70

Ukrainian did his best to change the subject, in order to lose his temptation of baiting Pyat. "I could do with a drink," he said.

"You usually could." Pyat disapproved of Makhno's habits.

Una was pleased with Makhno's self-control as he resisted any further mention of the twenty-five grams of cocaine found on Pyat while the militia was searching him. The soldiers had accepted his explanation that these were headache powders ·and had carefully set them aside, doubtless for their own use. Makhno and Una had been amused by such a turn of events but, for a while, just after they had been tied up in the truck, Pyat had wept. He still had some five grams hidden in the collar of his English shirt: just under his nose, as it were, but at this moment totally unattainable.

"The Cossacks aren't cowards, at least!" Pyat returned grumpily to the earlier point.

"No," said Makhno. "They seek out the highest possible authority and then fight for it to the death." Actually, he shared a great deal of Pyat's romanticism where Cossack ideals were concerned. A number of renegades had fought with him at Ekaterinburg and elsewhere, though at least half his officers had been Jewish intellectuals who had recognised in him a tactician of almost preternatural genius. Because Makhno had objected to Grigorieff's pogroms the anarchist had shot down Grigorieff while the nationalist hetman's followers looked on. A little later he had gently disbanded the nationalist army as being of no use to him because it had 'absorbed inhumane habits of thought and action'. That had been the day before he had carried the black banner against the combined forces of Trotsky's reds and Krasnoff's Don Cossack whites, when the anarchist army, outnumbered four to one, had scattered its enemy so thinly along the banks of the Pripet, and later the Donets, that since then neither Reds nor Whites had ever considered a further strike against the Ukrainian heartland. Nowadays, of course, Makhno was *persona non grata* in Kiev. His sense of history gave him an ironic perspective on the situation. He had expected nothing else. For the past twenty-five years he had lent his energies to half-a-dozen successful revolutions and a dozen failures, such as the recent ones in Canada, Yucatan and Somalia. It had only been to please Una, who had looked him up in Paris during one of his three-month benders, that he had become involved in supporting the Bohemian anarcho-communists who only a week before had threatened Prague under his leadership. But the whole army had been betrayed, in classic manner, by authoritarian socialists. Bolsheviks had all destroyed the anarchists in an ambush in the Ruthenian Carpathians, near the Veretski Pass. There had been nothing for it but to try to take what was left of their light armour through Hungary and seek refuge in Vienna, but the Bolshevists had somehow found an airforce and seven aerial cruisers and had bombed the rest of the army to bits. About fifty survivors had split up in order to cross the Austrian border, but Una, Pyat and Makhno had been recognised and turned back, having to take the train via Brno to Passau, where the Bolshevists, temporarily in control, had caught them. Una knew that their return to Prague as prisoners was bound to embarrass someone, so there was a chance that they would be 'lost'—shot or let go. It was a fifty-fifty chance. And if Lobkowitz was given the opportunity to save them, it would embarrass him and put him in an extremely difficult position, if he appeared to favour them.

Una freed herself at last. Lobkowitz hardly knew Makhno or Pyat and so their chances were better than hers. Travelling alone she would have more flexibility and therefore more hope of escape. She stood up. She spoke a little shakily as she peeled back the canopy, waiting for the truck to slow.

"Good luck." She unhooked her tape-player from her belt. She checked the batteries. It was still surprising that the militia had left the unfamiliar-looking machine with her. Perhaps they had decided it was a booby-trap. She

PRINZ **LOBKOWITZ**

switched on. Richard Hell was singing *You Gotta Lose*. "It's painful unless it's loud," she said. But she failed to get the volume very much higher. It served its purpose, however, drowning out Pyat's protests and causing the truck to slow.

She slipped through the curtain.

Time for a new temporary role, she thought.

## 2

### KITTY-KOLA: A CORRECTION

*Our attention has been drawn to an article entitled Sudan in Ferment in your issue of Dec. 29. In this article you refer to 'Egypt's plagiaristic Kitty-Cola.' We would point out that 'Kitty-Kola' has no connection whatever with Egypt. 'Kitty-Kola' is a speciality soft drink marketed by this company, and licences for its preparation and sale are granted to bottlers after their application has been approved. The Kitty-Kola Co. Ltd., of London, is associated with another English company which has now been established over 100 years and there is certainly no connection whatsoever with Egypt.*

*'Kitty-Kola' is a drink formulated here in England which is rapidly gaining acceptance on world markets. It is all part of this country's export drive and of our efforts to keep overseas markets which have been traditionally this country's for many, many years.*

LETTER: Picture Post, 1 March 1952

---

IT WAS 1952 according to Una's newspaper and 1976 according to Nick Lowe, who was singing *Heart of the City* on her Vidor portable radio as she raised its lid and slid back in her deckchair, positioned to face Bognor's doubtful ocean. Jerry, that eternal spirit of seaside holidays past, came limping over the shingle towards her, his scrawny body bright red and peeling, his peculiar trunks threatening to slip over his hips.

"Blimey! Hot enough for you?"

Una pushed her sunglasses onto her forehead. "You didn't get burned like that on any British beach. Not in May you didn't."

"I'm not burned!" He was indignant. "I'm tanning. What's that row?" He nodded at the Vidor.

She turned it off. "The future. Do you want to get me an ice-cream? What flavours do they have?" She reached into her beach-bag for her purse.

"Flavours? They might have strawberry. But it's probably only vanilla."

"The newspaper was right."

"Eh?"

"Get me a wafer, will you?"

He was glad to go. He returned with two hard blocks of ice-cream sandwiched between wafer biscuits. Austerity, she thought, took some getting into. She wished she was back in the Balkans where life, at least, was interesting. She looked to left and right at deckchairs and British bathers. This was Jerry's nightmare, not her own.

He kneeled beside her, licking the ice-cream, looking craftily out to sea.

"Well," she said. "What is it? You arranged to meet, don't forget."

"Oh, yeah." He was looking younger and weaker, as if time were running backwards in him and draining him as it did so. "My mum said I ought to join the Home Guard."

"You want me to get you out of some sort of domestic row? Or military service?"

"I'm stuck here, Una. I've lost all my old power. I don't think you realise . . ."

"I can't change the megaflow."

The word was only dimly familiar to him. "It's ever since mum died."

"Your mother's still alive. I saw her over near the entrance to the pier."

"That's what's wrong."

"Retrogressive tendencies, eh?" She shook her head. "You always had them. But you never came this far back before—and not on this line. Do you know there's never been a second world war here?"

He was disbelieving. "Then why are we putting up with all this bloody austerity?"

"We never got over the General Strike. There's nothing much wrong with the economy. It's supporting the Empire. This is a sort of punishment on the working classes."

"No!"

"There are pros and cons," she told him.

"Cor!" He was impressed. "What can you do to get me out of it?"

"I don't think you've got the moral rigour to do it," she said. "You're not even a force for Chaos any more. You've become a victim, Jerry. Once . . ."

He smirked.

It made her laugh. "I'll do my best. Is your mate Collier around?"

"In London. His mum and dad aren't going anywhere this year."

She closed the lid of the Vidor and fastened the catches, replacing it in her bag. She took out a strange Baedeker and turned to the timetables at the back.

---

## 3

### WILL THE FRENCH HOLD?

*There is therefore grave danger that the French, losing every year the equivalent in officers of a complete promotion from their military college of Saint Cyr and 5,000 boys from every corner of France, deserted as they think by their natural allies, the British and the Americans, threatened as they think by a revived Wehrmacht, may pull out of Indo-China and bring their battle-trained divisions home to watch the Rhine. But if they do, Korea will look like a tactical exercise, and Malaya a piece of boy-scouting. Indo-China, as de Lattre told the Americans, is as important as the Battle of the Bulge in 1944. If it falls, Communism within a few short months could be battering at Suez and Australia. The Diggers might hold out: how about Farouk?*

ARTICLE: Picture Post, 1 March 1952

---

THERE HAD TO be an alternative, thought Una, to Disco Fever on the one hand and the Red Army Ensemble on the other. She drove the hearse as fast as she dared; up past the West London Crematorium and round the corner into Ladbroke Grove. Behind her something in the elaborate coffin grumbled and squeaked. Jerry never

travelled well, even when she was trying to help him through the early seventies and into the middle of that decade where, everything being equal, he could rest up for a bit. Most likely, she thought, he was objecting to the fact that the hearse was a converted Austin Princess and not the Daimler he had asked for. If he went on like this, however, she would have to give up all her promises and bury him in the country. Somewhere near Godalming, she thought viciously. But she hadn't the heart for it.

Or the sea, she thought. Not for the first time.

She groped on the seat beside her for her half-eaten apple. There was nothing harder, she reflected, as she speeded up past a march of Radical Social Workers, for the

77

imaginative person to imagine than an unimaginative person. Consequently the paranoid ascribed every Machiavellian motive to the dullest, least inventive people. Those least capable of subtle malice were those most often credited with it. The time dwellers had to learn such things early. Too often metaphysics got you and then you were lost. It was very much like a drug experience, she supposed. But that was more in Jerry's line than hers. She would have to ask him when he woke up.

She went past Ladbroke Grove tube station, past the Kensington Palace Hotel on the one side and The Elgin on the other, past the new housing development standing on the site of the Convent of the Poor Clares, past Blenheim Crescent, where Jerry's mum had lived, and parked near the corner, just before Elgin Crescent. From the house opposite came Shakey Mo Collier and three of his ageless friends, in black leather, studs, silver, and street ephemera, members of the pop group Motorhead. In the lead, his features beaming with somewhat generalised good-will behind mirror shades, was Lemmy. He pushed his hair back from his ears and lit a cigarette. "Bloody hell," he said. "Is this it, then? Is it?"

"It's all yours." Una found herself warming to the musician. He reminded her of Jerry. "Is the hole ready?"

Mo interrupted. "I dug it myself. Are you sure he won't—you know—cough it?"

"He can't," said Una. "Can he?"

---

# 4

## LINER TO MARS

*We've seen how short-sighted these particular prophets were. Is the same story going to be repeated when, some time during the next fifty years, we begin the exploration of space? Most scientists who've made a serious study of 'astronautics' agree that we'll ultimately be able to build spaceships, but probably few consider that they'll be of much more than scientific value. We'll be able to send small expeditions to the Moon and planets, at very great expense—but as for large-scale space-flight and the colonisation of the planets, that belongs strictly to the realms of 'science-fiction'. So say the pessimists—and we propose to ignore them. It may take a hundred years, it may take a thousand—but, ultimately, men will lift their commerce into space as they've lifted it into the air. The liners of the future, homeward bound from Mars or Venus, will link our Earth with the new worlds that now lie waiting for the first human footsteps.*

ARTHUR C. CLARKE: Picture Post, 1 March 1952

---

"EVERY FUTURE WE inhabit is someone else's past," said Una as she and Catherine unpacked the picnic. "God, how I yearn for the mindless present. When you were a kid. Do you remember?"

"Do you? I've got a lot of different memories. It's what happens to you."

Una nodded and began to peel the sealing strip from the small jar of Beluga caviar they had brought, while Catherine buttered slices of Ryvita. They had parked their orange Mobylette-50s by the gate of this Cumbrian field and were seated in the long grass by the river. Overhead was a willow. To their left was a small stone bridge, thick with weeds and flowers and scarcely ever used. Behind them and ahead of them were rolling, vari-coloured summer hills, their contours and buildings unchanged since the 17th century. The women took deep breaths of rich air and swatted at midges and wasps. As often happened in this part of England, summer had come early and would be short. They were making the most of it. It was one of the few parts of the world where both of them could feel completely at ease. Fifty miles or so away, on the coast, the great nuclear reactors seemed to guard their security, as timeless as the rest of the landscape. Una, so used to impermanence, to plastic vistas, to all kinds of physical and social permutations, found herself incapable of imagining any radical change to this world. They had built a six-lane motorway through it, and that had only enhanced it, added a dimension. She smiled to herself. She had thought the same of the Sussex downs, once, without realising that that was where she was. Was it a state of mind which imposed tranquility upon a landscape, after all? Was it the only salve offered to the wounded romantic imagination? She had always preferred hills and mountains to valleys and plains. When she was in low country she always felt the urge to run off someone's cattle.

"There's an inevitability to linear thinking that sometimes brings me down a bit." Catherine mused. "Do you remember that time in Bombay? Or wherever. The future. No, it couldn't have been Bombay? Angkor Wat? Anuradhapura? One of those old cities. They had created a huge future and then it had deserted them. Is that what happened? A divergence of some kind? Where did they go? All these mysterious monuments scattered about the world. Monuments to literal-mindedness."

"And the literal-minded, in turn, think that people from space built them." Una was amused. "There's an irony."

"They'd never get it." Catherine pulled back her blouse and bared her breasts to the sun. "Ah. That's better. The only invasion from space I care about is the one that turns me nice and brown."

"It's a very simple form of pragmatism," said Una. She hitched up her summer frock and put her feet in the water. "But that's fair enough. We are on holiday."

"Which reminds me. How's Jerrry?"

Una wished that Catherine hadn't raised the subject. "Lying low."

"In cold storage is he? That makes a change."

Una had forgotten how little disturbed Catherine could be where Jerry was concerned. Catherine believed Jerry to be immortal.

Her feet still in the water she turned at the waist and laid a lip on Catherine's nipple.

Catherine stroked Una's hair.

"You must be tired of playing Jerry's role," she said sympathetically.

Una rolled on to her back. "Shall we buy a place here? A retreat?"

"There's no such thing, love. Once you own it, it stops being a retreat. You know that as well as I do." Catherine found her friend's hand. "Sorry if I upset you. I didn't mean . . ."

"You don't understand," said Una.

"Does one have to? I can't believe much in understanding. I do believe, though, in sympathy and comfort. In enthusiasm. What is understanding? It's translation. And you always lose something when you translate. Don't you?"

"But you have a rough idea of what I'm going through."

"Sort of," said Catherine. She laughed. "No."

Much to Una's own relief, she laughed in return.

---

## 5

### "IF ONLY MY NAME WAS DENIS"

*To score double centuries, to man a frontier-post in Mexico, to pilot a Space-fleet to Mars—these are games popular with every boy of every age. And it is natural and right that this should be so. Tales of sport and adventure and excitement fire a boy's imagination; they help him to see the world in a fresh and vivid way; they enlarge his horizon, and inspire his ideals. Yet—it cannot be denied—a boy's longing for adventure and excitement may often cause great and reasonable anxiety. Adventurousness may be turned to violence, excitement to cruelty by a variety of vicious influences. And here cheap second-rate comic-strips are much to blame. They warp and distort a boy's sense of values and give him a false outlook on life; under their influence he fancies himself a hero, a superman; someone who escapes responsibility and seeks refuge in fantasy. It remains the prime object of EAGLE to change all that; and (adapting the famous phrase) to see that 'the Devil does not have all the exciting comics'. Here no creed of violence is preached; no tawdry morality or cheap sensationalism or worship of the superman ever appears. For*

---

MAJOR NYE SAT on a stool outside his shed, grunting as his daughter Elizabeth grew bright red and tugged at his left gumboot. "Sorry about this," he said.

Una and Catherine said in concert: "Can I help?"

"It's okay," said Elizabeth. "Awkward buggers, wellies. Sorry, dad." She winked at her friends. "He hates me swearing."

"I shouldn't," he said. "Do enough of it myself." He rose in his thin socks. "What do you think of the patch now?" He regarded, with some satisfaction, his vegetable gardens. "We're almost entirely self-sufficient, you know. Apart from tobacco. But that's not really any good for you, anyway, is it? Come the revolution, we'll be okay."

Una remembered a thousand famines and gasped.

"You all right, Mrs P?" He put his hand on her arm. "Trod on a stone? Put the kettle on, Liz, there's a good girl. We'll have some tea."

Elizabeth shrugged. "Come and help me, Cathy."

Una and Major Nye stood alone in the garden. From an upstairs window a pale, forgotten face regarded them with miserable and imperfect knowledge. "I had planned to retire completely," said the major. "But what with kids to educate and the wife's doctors, and the value of the pension going down every year . . ."

"We're the only ones Prinz Lobkowitz trusts," said Una. "If you can get Makhno out of prison in Australia I think it would do a lot of good. The charge was trumped up, wasn't it?"

"I wouldn't go as far as that. But I've looked at the file. A lot of circumstantial evidence, certainly. We could re-open the case.''

''And release him.''

''I think so.'' Major Nye sat down on the stool again and put his feet into carpet slippers. He lifted a boot and began to bang it against a nearby step. ''I saved some radishes for you.''

''Lovely. The conference is to be held in September. In Trieste.''

''Best time of year for Trieste.'' He began to roll himself a cigarette. ''I should think the Jugoslavs are happy about that. Not so far to go for them.''

''They're hardly playing an important role. They've been more or less neutral, along with Ukrainia. Lobkowitz hopes for a Pan-Slavic Treaty, to include the Russian states.''

''They've always been a bit stand-offish, haven't they?''

''But it isn't important. Makhno is still very much respected in Ukrainia, even if he isn't liked. He was never a natural politician.''

''That's obvious. Fancy trying to start an anarchist uprising in Queensland!'' Major Nye lit his cigarette, puffing vigorously. ''That's what I call Quixotic, Mrs P. Eh?''

''Well, optimistic, anyway.''

''I've heard that Makhno wasn't too pleased with you, however.'' Major Nye squinted back at the house, but the face had withdrawn.

''Not Makhno. You're thinking of Pyat.''

''You know my nick-name for that one?''

''No.''

''Squash.''

''Swede?''

''What? Oh, not the turnip sort. The game. Fives. Get it? Why does he call himself by a number? Is it an old code-name? Those Russians change their names at the drop of a hat.''

''I don't know what his real name is.'' Una smiled. ''It's strange I never wondered. Colonel Five. Five what?''

"Five lives," he said, "at least."

"Five lies, in his case. He's not a colonel, of course. I don't think he's ever served in a war. Not voluntarily, at any rate. He's from Kiev. An engineer or something. Born in Minsk. His family—his mother, at least, went to Tsaritsyn where he spent his early childhood. Later the pair of them turned up in Kiev. I think that's where he met Makhno."

"A funny pair."

"He doesn't like Makhno a bit. But he sticks close to him. Familiarity is a form of security, after all."

"So Makhno is still friendly to you."

"As always. That doesn't mean he listens to me. And

I'm not going to represent you this time, major. I did it once, for reasons of my own."

"Oh, quite. No. All I want you to do is brief him. I'm sure he'll support Lobkowitz. They're both anarchists."

"Lobkowitz is a pacifist. Makhno isn't."

"I suppose it was simple-minded of me to link them in that way."

From the house Elizabeth called that tea was ready. Major Nye guided Una towards the side door, past the empty stables. "You must come in June. It's the best time to see our place."

"Maybe it's a diminutive," she said. "Of fifty. Pyatdyaset."

"Why fifty?"

"No reason. It's just associations of my own. I'm rambling. Mozart sonatas. God, I hate the fifties."

"You'll be out of them soon." They reached the kitchen. "Think of me. Stuck in 'em for God knows how long. Borderland years for me. For you they are merely the badlands. To be crossed quickly and forgotten about. They've done me in, Mrs Persson." He reached to open the door into the sitting room. "I assure you I don't like them any more than you."

For the first time, she realised the extent of his dignity.

It was these old men she admired most. Those who had suffered so much and still kept their faith. They were braver than Makhno in many ways. But Makhno was one of them. And perhaps more attractive.

In the old couch Bishop Beesley leered at her.

"I don't believe you've met our vicar," said Mrs Nye from her invalid chair.

# 6

## S. AFRICA SEEKING LEG IRONS

*Tenders have been invited by the South African Police for the supply of 200 leg irons, apparently as the result of a ban imposed by the United States government last month on the export of 'torture' equipment to the republic. The exact specifications of what the police need are on file with the Director of State Purchases in Pretoria. They are to be marked 'SAP'—South African Police—and supplied with two keys. Emphasis is placed in the tender document on a 'secure system'.*

Daily Telegraph, 20 July 1978

"THE FRENCH CAN'T help their Classicism any more than the Italians can control their Romanticism. Look at those poor French horror comics. Their sex magazines. Look at Le Drugstore! And so it is with politics. They must always embrace some classical, unambiguous cause. They become Marxists." It was autumn in the Luxembourg Gardens and, as always, the only time they were at all atmospheric. A few leaves disgraced the orderly paths or lay, willy-nilly, on the gravel. Makhno stiffened his back to gain height, but he remained significantly shorter than Una. On the other hand; his girl-friend, Maxime, was diminutive. She wore her camel-hair coat as if it were a uniform. Her small, fierce face peered at Una from beneath a defiant orange 'punk' coiffure. She gave exactly the same attention to Una as she did to Makhno. And she said nothing. Occasionally she would light a cigarette with an old-fashioned Polish petrol lighter, using energetic, economical movements. If Una smoked a cigarette, Maxime would light it. Makhno was smoking papyruska cigarettes from a box inscribed with a representation of Ilya Moromyets and other Kievan legendary heroes. They were a commercial Russian brand called Vogatyr, made in Moscow. He was completely grey now and his face, although a little corroded from his drinking, was still humorous and attractive. He had the same sardonic manner, the same look of stocky integrity. He was nearly seventy, in exile in Paris again, having found the role of Bohemian diplomat too much at odds with ideals which, as he said, had become physical as well as mental habits, so that his very presence in conferences made other people uncomfortable. He wore an old-fashioned Norfolk jacket, plus-fours and his favourite pair of English riding boots which he had picked up in some South American war. He held the tube of the Russian cigarette upwards and at an angle away from his hand. The smoke, drifting through the clear air, made Una feel at once nostalgic and wary. Her romance with the various Slav revolutions had brought her too much pain. It had been a century full of fire and she would look on it with nostalgia, if the memory lasted at all.

"Pure, classical Marxism," murmured Makhno. "Not the rough-edged vulgar Russian kind. Closer to the Chinese, of course, with whom the French have such an affinity. And they have made me a hero!" He dropped the cigarette. "They have almost convinced me that I am 'really' a Marxist. Poor old Kropotkin. He wasn't quite mad enough, was he?"

"You're becoming a racist," said Una.

"I'm Ukrainian. All Ukrainians are racists. Racism is an honourable form of logic pre-dating psychology as a useful way of rationalising prejudice."

Bishop Beesley, in gaiters and frock-coat, and Miss Brunner, in severe St Laurent tweed, approached them through the stiff, Parisian trees. The co-conspirators were arm in arm. They waved when they sighted Makhno's party.

"Hi," said the bishop, perhaps not sure where he was. "How goes it?"

Maxime slowly turned her eyes on him. Then she regarded Miss Brunner. It was as if she absorbed their essence. Miss Brunner looked uncomfortable and then curious. She smiled at Maxime. "Hello, dear. I don't know you, do I?"

Maxime looked to Makhno.

87

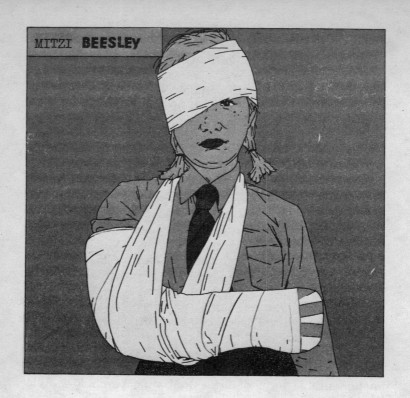

MITZI BEESLEY

"This is Maxime," he said. "We are married."

"Oh, congratulations." Bishop Beesley put a fat hand towards the girl, who flinched. He looked at it, perhaps detecting a trace or two of chocolate on the pink flesh, and began to suck it before he drew a red and white spotted hankerchief from the pocket of his coat and wiped the hand carefully. Meanwhile Miss Brunner appeared to have sidled between Makhno and Una and threw a cloud of some Gerlaine or other about them all. "Darling Nestor!"

"What?" Makhno coughed. "Are you emissaries from the Germans?"

"Certainly not. We are tourists."

"Trapped," added the bishop, "like you."

"We're not trapped." Makhno grinned. "We're communards, all of us."

"Splendid," said Miss Brunner. "We were hoping you were." She bit her lip; looking up as a flight of Prussian Starfighters came honking and wailing through the misty morning. "Bombers?"

"They only observe us. We're an independent city. Technically, we're not even under siege. Technically, there's no German blockade." Una watched Miss Brunner who hefted her handbag on her arm and glanced at Bishop Beesley who drew a small Browning automatic from his pocket and pointed it at Makhno. Miss Brunner produced her old Smith and Wesson .45 from the bag.

Nestor Makhno took out his cigarette case and offered a Vogatyr to the company. "Is this an assassination?"

"Justice," said Miss Brunner.

The scene fractured and Una, Makhno and a frowning Maxime stood at the crest of a hill, looking down on the white road winding across the yellow Ukrainian steppe. There were no houses to be seen. Behind them, three ponies, furnished for war, cropped at grass. Makhno returned his field glasses to their case. "We had best make for the railway station," he said. "It's too far to ride."

They mounted the ponies, but, even as they began to trot forward, the scene melted and became a town in flames. Nationalist bandits were looting it. It was the time of the retreat from Minsk. Makhno drew his revolver, firing into the air. "Stop!" He moved round in his saddle and shot a looter wearing an army greatcoat and a sailor's cap. The man began to cough and searched for his own gun amongst the knives and swords and cartridge belts hung about his chest and waist. He fell on his knees and collapsed to one side before he had sorted through the collection and discovered that his holster had moved round to the small of his back.

Two armoured cars moved through the smoke and the crowd. A green flag waved from a mast on the leading vehicle. The street was mud. The noise of mortars and

human beings mingled into one appalling scream. Una was about to wheel her mount when a silence fell and the ponies were plodding knee-deep through snow. Una shivered. The fracture had saved them from Miss Brunner and Bishop Beesley but it could have sent them into stasis. In this primordial snow they must soon freeze. It would mean the end of a whole cycle of consequences. She began to feel the familiar lethargy and prepared herself for the fate which must sooner or later befall all temporal adventurers.

"Mush!"

It was Jerry, driving a team of dogs, a corpse-shaped bundle before him on his sleigh. He was dressed in white furs and looking his most handsome. "Want a lift?"

90

Makhno put fresh shells into his revolver. "Where are you going?"

"Does it matter?" Una dismounted and plunged through the snow towards the sleigh which became a small boat in which Jerry and Catherine, dressed as seaside Pierrots, manned two sets of oars and at the same time stretched to where she stood waist-deep in the sea, trying to get to them. Una herself was dressed as Harlequin and her vision was impaired by her mask. She felt a strange, melancholy lust.

"Quick," said Catherine. "There's still time, Una. Quick."

But Una was losing it. She knew. Memories dissipated. Identity failed. She was still in her Harlequin set as she stumbled up the yellow beach of some Indian Ocean island, weeping for rest. Desperate for consolation.

## 7

### COMPUTERS PICK LIKELY 'SUICIDES'

*Computers can predict suicide attempts much more accurately than human therapists because they have no hesitation in asking blunt questions, according to a series of experiments by two psychiatrists at Wisconsin University Medical School. When hundreds of depressed patients were interviewed by a computer . . . three suicide attempts were accurately predicted. The two doctors had failed to predict any of them . . . In the first part of the interview, the computer would win their confidence with such morale-boosting remarks as: 'You're a pro at using the terminal.' Then it became blunter with such questions as: 'What are your chances of being dead from suicide one month from now?'*

Daily Telegraph, 20 July 1978

"WHAT ARE THESE new Americans who have made of tautology a substitute for literature? Who celebrate the euphuism as an art-form? Who take crude peasant prejudice and elevate it, placing it on par with Emerson or

Paine? What are these babblers, so free to debase the Word? Who employ the corrupt terminology of the encounter group in all their dealings?'' Professor Hira held the board against the window and reached for the hammer Una passed him. ''Eh?''

''I'm sure I don't know, darling? I'm not a great reader,''

''Do you have to be? You should wear something more practical.''

''I like satin. It's cool. Do you think the Dacoits will attack before help comes?'' She adjusted a pink strap.

He scratched his hair-line, just where his turban touched his forehead. ''We can't take chances. There is nothing worse than an Indo-Chinese pirate. You must shoot yourself, of course, if they land.'' She turned back to look out to sea. The sails of the junks seemed no closer and the smoke of the white steam yacht which appeared to lead them was, if anything, closer to the horizon. The little Brahmin knocked an inexpert nail into the board and then made his way cautiously down the ladder. The main settlement of Rowe Island was below them: a group of stone and stucco buildings which had housed the mine-managers, their employees and the few traders who had found it worthwhile to set up shops and hotels here. Professor Hira's house had once been the control shack for the airship field. The steel, triangular mast was still there, but no ships had called in years, since the mining of phosphates had become unprofitable. The Malays and Chinese labourers had been the first to go. There had been some attempt by the mine-owners to turn the place into a resort, but it was too far from anywhere else in the world to attract more than a few of those who genuinely sought a remote haven. Now it was a sort of R&R base for members of the Guild, being away from all shipping routes. The one hotel was run by Olmeijer, the fat Dutchman, who for some reason found it convenient to serve Guild people, but Olmeijer had made his annual journey to Sarawak, to see one of his several families, and would not be back for two

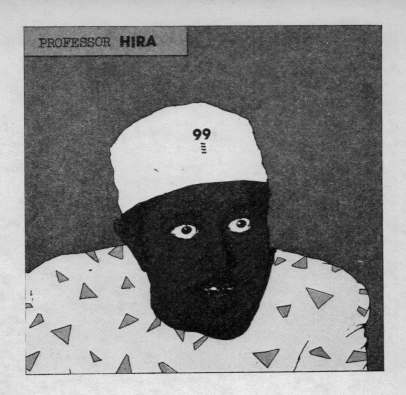

PROFESSOR **HIRA**

weeks. Hira and Una were presently the only inhabitants.

"There's nothing at all here for them." Hira squinted out to sea. "Could they be after us?"

"What would they want?"

"They could be linears, out to destroy our base. It wouldn't be the first time. Remember what happened in 1900, at the Centre?"

"It was one of the very first and oldest bases. We never made the same mistake. That Centre was shifted into the Palaeozoic. Or was it the Devonian?"

"Don't ask me. We have different terms for the time cycles. But they're about as vague as yours." He heard a familiar coughing from the sky and looked up to point

towards the silhouette of a cream-coloured Dornier DoX banking over the top of a cloud and heading clumsily towards the island. "We all know who that must be."

"I wish to god he'd get a better bloody plane."

"It suits his sense of history."

The huge white aircraft floundered lower, only half its engines firing at any one time. It had a grubby, under-used look to it.

"I suppose," said Una, hitching up her long dress,

94

"we'd better get down to the harbour before the pirates."
She had noticed that the yacht had picked up speed. She
heard a distant rumble. "They've got a Bofors. They're
firing at the plane."

It was impossible to tell if the plane were hit. From
somewhere near its tail, a Browning M1917-A1 began to
fire. The junks retaliated, with every kind of light
weaponry, but principally, if Una's ear were in, with near-
useless Ingram M10s.

"At least they're a bit more up to date," said Una. They had reached the ramshackle outskirts of the settlement and were running over distorted flagstones towards the harbour. "But at least we can be certain of one thing. We're in a fault of some sort. Maybe even a loop."

"It's better than being frozen," said the Brahmin.

Una's memory became vague again. At least she still knew enough to understand that there were no such things as paradoxes and that ambiguities sustained and enriched the basic fabric of human life; that Time was a notion and nothing more; and therefore could neither be challenged, nor overwhelmed: merely experienced.

Death, of course, was real enough, when it came. She looked nervously towards the yacht which appeared to be sporting a Hudson's Bay Company flag. She could easily spot the Dacoits on the deck. They were training the Bofors towards the harbour itself. She thought she saw the glint of a bishop's mitre on the bridge.

Whining and grunting intermittently, the DoX flew low overhead, its wings swaying, turned almost directly over the yacht and came in to land on the oily waters of the harbour, bouncing dangerously on its heavy floats. The engines continued to miss as a figure emerged from the cabin and stood on the float, signalling to them.

"We're going to have to swim for it," said Professor Hira removing his beautiful silk coat.

"Bugger," said Una. She stripped off her pink satin evening dress and in nothing but her camisole returned gingerly to the water.

Shakey Mo Collier helped her crawl onto the float. His long hair fell about his yellow, seedy face. There was a black Burmese cheroot in one corner of his mouth. He wore huge mirror-shades which gave him something of an insectile look. He was dressed as Captain Fracasse, although the costume was filthy and so torn as to be barely recognisable. "We were on our way to Australia," he explained, "when we got your call. Is that the Teddy Bear firing at us?"

"It must be," said Una. "The last time I was on it was for the concert party. Do you remember?" Dripping, she climbed into the cabin. Frank and Jerry, in identical flying gear, sat at the twin controls.

"Remember?" said Mo, reaching out a hand towards Professor Hira. "I haven't had a moment to bloody change, have I?"

Frank looked round at her and licked chemically-reddened lips. "Cor! Me first," he said appreciatively.

Jerry's voice was remote. "No time." An automatic arm stretched towards the throttle. "Taking her up." There was flak now, and spray, as shells struck the water near them. The plane lurched, bounced, slewed round and had to be straightened out. Then they were taking off, the sound of the inefficient engines drowning the sound of maniac gunfire which burst from every ship in the pirate fleet.

They were back in the political arena with a vengeance.

---

## 8

### SIX LIFE SENTENCES FOR ANTI-ABORTION BOMB STUDENT

*A 'brilliant' science student, who carried out fire bomb attacks on people whose pro-abortion views 'sickened' him, was given six concurrent life sentences when he appeared at the Old Bailey yesterday. (He) made 'lethal and beautifully designed bombs which, by the grace of God, did not kill anyone,' said the Recorder of London Mr James Miskin Q.C. 'He took the view that those who support abortion are wrong. He has exhibited no remorse or any concern for his intended victims . . .' In a workroom at his home police found 'a mass of bomb-making equipment' and a diary in which he recorded his crimes. He had written about his urge to 'purge the land of evil' and of his 'noble mission' against abortion. Of the bomb intended to maim Mrs Lord, he said: 'I laughed to think of my own cunning in constructing it . . . I believe strongly that something should be done to remedy abortion. I am sickened by it and decided a campaign against those who preach the unwarranted murder of innocent children.'*

Daily Telegraph, 20 July 1978

"IT ONLY COSTS about £16.00 for the whole round trip," said Una as she followed Catherine into the back of the Daimler limousine. "Hardly any more than a taxi, these days." She smiled at the chauffeur who had turned his head and was giving both of them the eye. She smoothed chiffon. "Derry and Toms," she said. "In Kensington High Street. Do you know it?"

"Well . . ." He shrugged. "I know what you mean." he put the car into gear and drove round the corner into Campden Hill Road. "Is that where you want to go? I mean, the only place?"

"And back," said Una, "when we've done some shopping and had our tea. Isn't it lovely today?"

"Lovely," said the chauffeur.

"I'm so glad to be back." Una giggled at Catherine. "So much has happened!"

Catherine, looking a little wary, said: "Yes?"

"You think I've changed?"

"Sort of."

"I've given up everything. I've decided to be more feminine."

"You're always deciding that," said Catherine. She looked soberly at her own blonde frizz in the little mirror provided. Her make-up was fashionably extravagant: imitating the naïve almost as successfully as a Lowry, but with much more passion. She put her red lips together. "And usually at the wrong time."

Una's enthusiasm waned. She crossed her legs. "It's the only escape they leave open."

"They leave it open because they want you to take it."

"Fine. I want to take it."

"Fine." Catherine spoke cheerfully, frustrating Una.

"Well, what else can I do? I need the rest."

"You ought to find another way, dear. Or another chap."

"He's lovely, Major Nye."

"He's married to that poor old bag. And then there's Elizabeth. I mean, she'd be pissed off to say the least, if she found out. You can't screw fathers and daughters and get away with it." Catherine laughed coarsely. "Bloody hell!"

"It's not really like that." Una was offended. She regretted suggesting the trip.

The Daimler reached Kensington High Street and turned left. "I need to combine ideals with sex, that's my trouble."

"It's because you're so puritanical."

Una nodded.

"That's it," said the chauffeur. "Isn't it?"

"God help us!" Una was terrified as she stared out at the department store. "I hoped I was safe!"

"It changed ages ago. To Biba's first. Then to this." Catherine was sympathetic. "I thought you knew. I thought you were being satirical."

"How do you get to the roof garden?"

"You can't any more, I don't think. It's private."

"Get anything in there these days," said the chauffeur.

Una continued to stare in silence at the pale green, the faded gold, of the new Marks and Spencers.

---

# 9

## GIFT FROM QUEEN

*Seven deer, two stags, and five hinds—the Queen's jubilee year gift to the Canadian province of Nova Scotia—will be flown from Heathrow today.*

Daily Telegraph, 20 July 1978

---

BENEATH THE GREY Westway motorway, in the gloom of the half-ruined People's Theatre, peering out of

PIERROT

the rain through wire-netting, sat Jerry Cornelius, a crest-fallen white linen Pierrot. He hugged his cold, thin body. He whimpered as, from another bay, further west, came the giggling and wheezing of his half-cut mum enjoying an afternoon gin with Bishop Beesley in some corner or other. He knew Una was standing at the back of the stage, behind him. She sniffed. The railway sleepers used for seats had been set on fire and partially burned. The theatre was useless, filthy, incredible. The Pierrot suit was wet, as if Jerry had tried to run home through the rain and then turned back. This Sunday they had all been due to make their appearance here, in a version of the role made famous by Sarah Bernhardt almost a century before, as *Pierrot Mort*.

Jerry's white make-up had the flaky look of salt-flats suddenly inundated. It made him look infinitely aged as he eventually turned reddish eyes to acknowledge her. "I thought they'd turn up anyway," he said. "Did you bring your costume?"

"I left it at your mum's. Cathy's there."

"I know. She wouldn't come."

"She said."

"Thought it wasn't worth it. There was no cancellation announced. I mean. Are we troopers or aren't we."

"Troopers." Una offered him a packet of Black Cats as she came towards him. "Of some sort or other."

"What's the point of doing a play to celebrate the spirit of the theatre and then showing none of that spirit yourself." He took a cigarette.

"Do you want to put it on?"

"There were only about six people turned up and they went away when they saw what had happened. Bloody vandals. Who was it?"

"I think it was a rival political theatre group," she said. "That's what I heard. Marxists. They're very concerned about reaching the people in the correct way."

"Bloody communists. Worse than the church."

"Well, so they say."

"And they're bloody right."

"Why can't they leave us alone."

"It's not in their nature."

"Sod them all."

"No point in sulking, Jerry. Not if you're a trooper."

"I'm not going to be brave about it. That's unhealthy. It's better if I sulk."

She sat down at the hacked-about piano and played a chord. The sound was primaeval; terrifying. She couldn't stop it. It grew in the bay; it echoed through all the other bays, right down to the end, in Ladbroke Grove. It joined the noise of the cars above, the trains of the Metropolitan Line to the south; there was a sense of eternal syncopation. Jerry's face cleared. Una shook the piano. The sound continued to swell from it.

"That's great," said Jerry.

"It's cacophony."

"No it's not. Listen."

"I don't want to listen."

"Everything intersects."

"We all know that."

"This is the music of the lines. Not the spheres. Like knitting. Like a vast cat's cradle. Can you hear it all, Una?"

"Nothing but a horrible noise."

He sighed. "Maybe you're right. All we have is imagination. And that lets you down so often. Everyone has a different explanation."

"Can you suggest a universal one?"

"Music."

"What?"

"Nothing."

The smell of damp charcoal was getting to Una. "Shall we go and have a cup of coffee in the Mountain Grill? We'll be under cover most of the way. You won't get much wetter."

"If you like." He had stopped sulking and had become artificially compliant. He got up at once and followed her through the gap in the wire, round the corner into Portobello Road. The windows of the Mountain Grill were steamed up from the inside. Within, the usual cast looked at the newcomers. There was a row of tables against either wall. Each row contained five tables. At the end of the café was the counter with the till on it. Behind the counter was the kitchen. In the kitchen were the Cypriot proprietor, his wife and his father. They were cooking the food. A little boy and a little girl, the proprietor's children, were serving it. There was a smell of boiling potatoes. It dominated all the other smells. At the furthest table on the left row sat Miss Brunner, Bishop Beesley, Karen von Krupp, Frank Cornelius. At the next table down sat Shakey Mo Collier, Nestor Makhno, Maxime and Mrs Cornelius. At the third

102

table were Major Nye, Elizabeth Nye, Pip Nye and Captain Nye. At the fouth were William Randolph Hearst, Orson Welles, Alfred Bester and Zenith the Albino, all in evening dress. The fifth was empty and Jerry and Una sat down at it, facing one another. On Una's right (her back was to the moist window) the tables were occupied thus:

Table One: Nik Turner, Dave Brock, DikMik, Del Dettmar

Table Two: Simon King, Bob Calvert, Lemmy, Martin Griffin

Table Three: Pete Pavli, Adrian Shaw, Michael Moorcock, Simon House

Table Four: Steve Gilmore, Douglas Smith, Wayne Bardell, Graham Charnock

Table Five: Phil Taylor, Eddy Clarke, Catherine Cornelius, Harvey Bainbridge

"It's bloody full this afternoon," said Jerry. "It's a wonder there's any empty chairs at all."

"They're for absent friends."

"What is this? A private party?"

"We're just waiting for some transport." Jerry began to feel a comforting sentimentality.

"You'd better get something inside you," she said.

## —————————10—————————

### VISCOUNT'S SON 'PAID £70 FOR CHILD SEX'

*A Viscount's son, on a 'fantasy bandwagon' fed by child pornography for several years, told Manchester Crown Court yesterday that he had paid £70 for an introduction to 'child prostitutes' at their mother's flat. (He) was giving evidence at the trial of a mother of three who is accused of inciting one of her daughters to commit gross indecency with him. (She) pleaded not guilty to three charges—encouraging an indecent assault on a girl under 16, indecent assault, with two men, on a girl under 13; and with a man, inciting a girl of 10 to commit gross indecency with (him). (He) claimed that he was 'revolted and horrified' by the*

---

THEY WERE STILL in their uniforms as they left the tiny theatre and climbed into the back of the Ford Transit. Una crawled through to the driving seat and pulled off her Harlequin mask. Jerry and Catherine lay face forward on the mattress while Catherine unscrewed the top of a thermos. Una got the engine going and backed the van into the midnight street. Even as Catherine handed her the plastic cup of sweet tea Una said goodbye to Harrogate and took the A65, heading north. "Never again," she said.

"They were awful." Jerry held out his own beaker and let it be filled. "What did they expect."

"Follies," said Una. "I knew it."

"There's no audience for the traditional *Commedia dell' Arte*," said Catherine dutifully, dabbing some tea-stains from her frothy costume. "And Harrogate's where people retire. They're nostalgic for the seaside pierrots. That's what they were expecting. That's why they left, you know. They were disappointed, all those retired people. We have ourselves to blame."

"Old farts," said Jerry. "You can keep bloody Harrogate. Where to next?" He remembered. "Kendal?"

"We're booked in at the Community Hall, but I'm not sure we should carry on." Una handed the cup behind her. "London was okay because people are into that sort of thing now. But we're ahead of our time up here."

"That's not hard." Catherine was grim. "I'm pissed off and no mistake. I never wanted any part of this pretentious crap. I thought it was going to be like those old people expected—songs and dances and that." She had given up duty.

"There *are* songs and dances." Una was aggrieved. It was she who had talked them both into the venture.

"Not proper ones." Catherine turned over on her back and tried to get comfortable with her head on her suitcase. "This is worse than rep."

"It's what rep's all about." Jerry, who had had less theatrical experience, still found the whole travelling part of it romantic.

"But it isn't rep. It's—God knows what!" Catherine sniffed and shut her eyes.

"It's how rep started. This."

"It's self-conscious." She opened her eyes again. "Has anyone got a cigarette?"

Jerry went to his own grubby bag and found a tin. "Only these rotten Russian ones."

"They'll do." She lit a papyruska. "I like 'em." She was enjoying herself, testing her power. She knew that they were both trying to placate her. She continued her role. "Couldn't we try to pep it up next time. With some more contemporary material—or at least some nostalgia stuff— vo-di-o-do—you know. This is so old nobody can feel nostalgic for it!"

"That's the point. It's genuine rediscovery of dramatic ideas disused for a couple of hundred years. Well, a hundred—if you count Debureau and Les Funambules—"

"Which I do," said Catherine, taking an entirely different but equally aggressive tack.

"Some Good Companions we are," said Jerry unhappily. "This ain't rock and roll. It's Leonard Merrick."

"Who?" they said.

He smiled smugly. He began to remove his make-up. He seemed to be the only one who was enjoying himself.

They made their way into the Dales, down the dark, empty road towards Cumbria.

Somewhere beyond Ilkley, a Banning began to sound for a few seconds. Then the noise died.

Jerry was asleep. Catherine crawled into the passenger

seat and handed Una one of her brother's Russian cigarettes already lit. "Was that fighting?"

"There's an army near. Of some sort. But I don't think we should worry too much. I'm going to try to make for the old road, once we're past Kirby. Get into safe country."

Catherine nodded. "Good idea."

She began to doze.

She was wakened by the dawn and looked to see a disturbed, red-eyed Una, looking dreadfully pale in her red, green, blue and gold lozenge motley. "What's the matter?"

"I can't find the bloody road. I've looked and looked. It's not blocked or anything. I just can't find it."

They were on the motorway. "But we're in it." said Catherine. "It's over there. And there."

"We're going through it. But I can't get into it. I don't know what's wrong."

"Where are we heading?"

"Where else?" said Una. "The Lake District."

They had reached Grasmere and had stopped in the deserted car park next to Dove Cottage before Jerry woke up, looked out of the back windows of the Transit, saw grey stone and turned pale. "Oh, no."

"Don't blame me," said Una. "All roads lead to Wordsworth."

"What?"

"That's how it seems."

"I hate this bloody place."

"Why do you keep coming back to it then," said Catherine sardonically. "And you do, don't you?"

"Not voluntarily. I thought—Weren't we heading for Kendal? We've passed it."

"By-passed it, actually," said Una. She was grim. "We can't go back and we don't want to stay here. Where shall we head for?"

Catherine said: "Keswick's better than this."

"Yeah," said Jerry. "Keswick."

"Why not Scotland?" Una leaned on the steering wheel

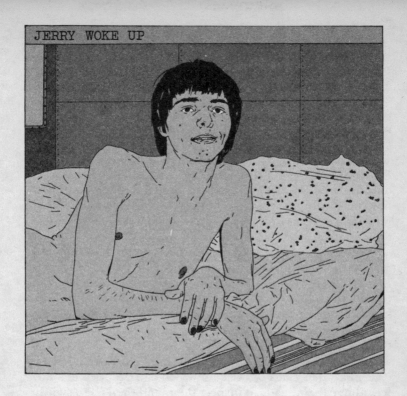

JERRY WOKE UP

and peered at the ruins of the Prince Charles Hotel beside the lake. "It's a free country, at least. And peaceful."

"Sort of peaceful. Is your pal still there? The anarchist?"

"There are lots of anarchists in Scotland now," said Una.

"You know the one I mean."

"Makhno should still be there. I'd like to look him up. He's getting on now, you know. Must be at least eighty."

"You wouldn't think it would you?" said Catherine salaciously. The older they got the more she fancied them.

From the lake emerged a peculiar submersible vehicle. It paused on the bank, throbbing. Its conning tower turned as if to watch them. A Browning M2 .50 took their range. Una started the old engine. "We can outrun that bastard if we're quick."

"Better do it, then," said Jerry. He unwrapped their only gun and wound down the side window even as he pushed Catherine into the back. The heavy Thompson .45 made him feel much better than it should have done.

The Transit lurched and Jerry fired a burst at the submersible more to startle it than anything else. The Browning did not fire back. Only when they were two hundred yards down the Scotland road did it begin to fire a few rounds, but it was evident that the crew—some kind of renegades—was conserving ammunition for defence rather than attack.

Jerry looked around him at ruined romance. The place had been the scene of five or six major battles between Black Watch divisions trying to establish themselves fresh territory since they had been driven out of Scotland and the local Cumbrian bandits who resented the incursion all the more since the Black Watch had little worth looting but their weapons.

By that afternoon they had crossed the border under the gaze of a small black patrol ship which had dropped to a few feet above their heads to inspect them and then risen swiftly as a sign that they could proceed.

By evening, after resting and eating, they could see sanctuary ahead as Glasgow's solid towers became visible above the mist.

"Shall we be staying?" asked Catherine of Una.

Una shook her head. "Not for long. The war is endless, you know. Someone has to carry on."

"You're sounding more like your old self," said Catherine approvingly.

"Well, one of them, at least," said Una.

Jerry rolled onto his side and began to snore.

# RECAPITULATION

## Every Gun Plays Its Own Tune

The Bishop and Mitzi
    Were on the rampage
She full of lust
    He full of rage
Looking for victims
    They hoped to convert
Stopped in the fifties
    And there found a cert . . .

They got me again
They got me again
Oh, shit, they got me again
I was holed out in 'fifty
And having some fun
When I heard Mitzi coming
Caught the sound of her gun

Bang-bang-bang
Here come the gang
Bang-bang-bang-bang-bang!

The Bishop and Mitzi
    They found him at last
Stuck in a time-slip
    On his way to the past
He cried out for mercy
    But they only laughed
As they took him in
    To remind him of sin . . .

They got me again etc.

Pierrot, poor Pierrot
Must become Harlequin
Learn about sin
Drugs, whisky and gin
Such a bad convert
That's the thing about him
He'll forget all his
Lessons in time . . .

They got me again etc.
Bang-bang-bang etc.


## Pierrot in the Roof Garden

I've climbed so high
I can't climb higher
I've reached the top
And have to stop
Sitting on the steeple
Like a silly little fairy
Goodbye Tom and Goodbye Derry
Goodbye sahib, hello effendi
Biba's bust and I'm so trendy
Marx and Spencer's fails to send me
I've a hole in my trousers
And a boil on my nose
But they won't catch me
With my teeth round a rose
My time's run out
I'm a senile ghost
Run-down loony
Who never signed up
Music box
They can't wind up
You should see
What I had lined up

It was sweet
And it was tasty
Lost the lot
By being too hasty
I don't care
I've reached the limit
You can keep the world
There's nothing in it
I'll just sit here
And eat my spinach
Waiting for
The thing to finish
Up above the moon
Is shining
As I squat here
Quietly whining
For Columbine
I still am pining
My reel is spinning
But I can't get
The line in
So I think I'll just
Crawl under this bush.


## Columbine's Carol

Sing for joy, we've met in time
Harlequin and Columbine
Praise the jolly myth of Yule
May good cheer forever rule
Fire doth blaze and snow doth fall
Peace on Earth for One and All
Holly shines and Ivy glows
Bunting from the roof-tops flows.
Sing for joy, we've met in time
Harlequin and Columbine.

In the bell-tower Pierrot kneels
Surrounded by the merry peels
Now they're singing ding-dong-dell
Send the sinners down to hell
Snow doth fall and fire doth blaze
Numbering poor Pierrot's days
Down the bell-rope he descends
Knowing he must face his end
Out into the graveyard white
Pierrot must embrace the night.

Sing for joy, we've met in time
Harlequin and Columbine
Sing for joy, we've met in time
Harlequin and Columbine

Surrounded by a Christmas throng
Pierrot sings a silent song
(Goodbye me and goodbye time
Goodbye lovely Columbine)
Falling snow and blazing fire
This is Pierrot's funeral pyre
Gone is laughter, gone is light
Pierrot must embrace the night.

Sing for joy, we've met in time
Harlequin and Columbine
Sing for joy, we've met in time
Harlequin and Columbine . . .

# 4. THE MINSTREL GIRL

# 1

## WHO TURNED THE COURTESY CAR INTO A HEARSE?

*ISIS provides accurate gyro-stabilised weapon-aiming for guns air-to-air and guns, rockets and bombs air-to-ground . . . The D-282 has the added facility of airspeed computation in the air-to-ground strike role. A unique feature of this equipment is roll stabilisation of the aiming mark, reducing tracking time by 50%. Incorporated within the single optical lens system is a fixed cross standby sight. ISIS is also designed to integrate with laser rangefinders and inertial navigation systems.*

Ferranti

"NUCLEAR FUSION WILL return our birthright to us. Melting our cities into the softer contours of our original hills; restoring our caves, our safe places, bringing back the radiant landscapes of the world before the Fall." Jerry Cornelius stepped carefully over the huge blown-up photograph of the three murdered killers covering the middle of the studio's floor. It was black and white. He was a ghost. She was surprised that she could still see him.

"If you could only guarantee it," she said. In the far corner of the studio Una shivered beside one of the old-fashioned floodlamps. She extended her palms towards the warmth. She wore a military greatcoat, spangled tights. He, on the other hand, wore a huge black fur coat, some kind of shako, jackboots, as if he hoped that these rather more substantial clothes would hold him together long enough to do whatever it was he had come here for. Sinuously, with all that was left of his old self-conscious grace, he came to a stop beside a tank of developing fluid. He pushed back his coat and eased his needle gun into the heavy holster at his hip. The outline of the holster spoiled the otherwise perfect symmetry beneath the fur. "Dusty roads," he murmured nostalgically.

Her shoulders slumped. "Why not?" Would he want her for his next victim?

There was a four by eight picture of a child pinned to the wall to her left; a naked blonde of about ten. He shrugged at it. "We bring them into the world and then they die."

She glanced at him in surprise. "Die."

He continued his approach. "Love can be found nowhere, these days, except in the ruins." His hands reached out.

"We're not there yet," she said.

His hands fell.

As if to apologise she said: "I cannot lose my belief in original sin. That is, I do think there are those who carry sin with them, who infect the rest."

"What would you do with them?" He seemed to be sulking.

"Them? I suspect I'm talking about myself."

"Why not."

It was twelfth night and he was on his way, he had told her, to the Hunt Ball. He had a pair of antlers in the parcel he had left by the door as he had entered to rescue her. Through the glass roof she watched the sky grow cold, yellow, and then black. She thought of sex and sighed.

She sighed again, regretfully. She could see his body trembling beneath his clothes. They were worlds apart.

(The girl's face came closer. He saw the eyes narrow and the mouth twist. She began to weep. He backed away, raising his hands defensively and shaking his head from side to side. The music started and the dance went on.

Let the good times roll.)

---

# 2

## WHERE IS THE KILLER WHO HATED REDHEADS?

*The Royal Air Force is currently undertaking studies on the use of the Hawk as a frontline operational aircraft in addition to its basic role as trainer. As Air Vice-Marshal Gilbert, Assistant Chief of Air Staff (Policy) put it to Interavia: 'We are well aware that the Hawk has an operational capability, in addition to training, and we are conducting studies to see to what extent the capability can be exploited under the operational conditions of the 1980s.' Among the tasks being looked at are ground attack, self-defence and air defence. A compact easily-maintained aircraft like the Hawk would clearly be an asset in any breakthrough situation in the NATO central region. It would be particularly effective against vehicles and thin-skinned armour columns which had advanced beyond the heavy anti-aircraft weapon support available in the existing front line.*

Interavia

---

"WE DO WHAT we do. We are what we are."

Maxime glanced up when she heard this. Her expression was one of amused irony. "Your voice has altered. It's deeper. Almost negroid, hein?"

"Oh shut up." Una freed herself from the grubby sheet and struggled towards the side of the vast Louis XIV bed. She reached it at last, rolled off, then crawled through the tangles of the sheepskin carpet to the mirrored wall to look at her seedy, youthful face. She stuck out her bruised red tongue and inspected the tiny sore on the tip. Naked, she turned and sat cross-legged with her back to the mirror, staring across the room to where Maxime, her faintly Asiatic face frozen in a frown, smoked a cigarette and smoothed her thin fringe down over her forehead. Behind the heavy yellow velvet curtains the dawn was breaking.

"Fuck!" said Una.

"Die," sighed Maxime. She stretched her muscular arms. "Is the world still there, this morning?"

Una got to her feet and, hunched with cold, padded for the door. "I used to enjoy it all. I used to love it."

Maxime's tight mouth smiled. "First the romance goes, then the love, then the lust. The innocent! The gangster!"

When the door closed, Maxime leapt from the bed and ran to the chair on which, last night, she had flung her party uniform.

Una watching her through the keyhole, experienced a faint stirring in the region of her pelvis. She had begun to develop a fear of individuals. Nowadays she could only

MARTINE

embrace causes. She knew it was a weakness, but history was not, at present, on her side.

## 3

*CAN TOO MUCH SEX PLAY LEAD TO MURDER?*
*One of the largest potential military markets during the next decade will be that for subsonic trainer/ground attack aircraft. While estimates vary from source to source, a reasonable assessment of the demand is that about 6,000 aircraft will be needed to replace existing types in countries outside the United States and the East Bloc.*
                                                                Interavia

"IT IS THE disordered mind which detects order everywhere", Prinz Lobkowitz held her tightly in his grey arms, looking down at her head through fine, fading irises as he stroked her hair. "The schizoid brain seeks desperately for systems, the paranoid produces patterns from the most unlikely sources. The mad eye selects only what it wishes to see—proof of political plots, evidence of interstellar visitation, moral corruption in any given society. The evidence is not presented to us in linear form, you see, and cannot be read as we read lines of print. The secret is to make no specific selection."

"And go mad," said Una.

"No, no, no. And learn to love the world in all its aspects."

"Even cancer?"

"Love and cancer are scarcely compatible. But you could say that what we call 'cancer' has a perfect right to exist."

"We'd all die," she said. She broke away from him.

"Nonsense. We'd all experience miracle cures." He was hurt by her action. He began to roll down his sleeves, glancing round him at the abandoned surgery in the hope that she would not see his tears.

She moved a step or two towards him. His body was stiffer than it had been, his tone was over-controlled. "Shall I see you tonight, Una?"

"No," she said. "I can't come."

The room shook. An explosion somewhere. The first for a long time. A tray of instruments tumbled to the floor. He picked up his jacket from the threadbare carpet, holding back a leaning screen with his other hand. She sat on the edge of the leatherette inspection couch and combed her hair. "What about art?" she said. "That orders things, surely? At best."

"But at best it doesn't deny the rest of the evidence." He buttoned his jacket and found his homburg where it had fallen behind the doctor's desk. The doctor's skeleton lay clean and slumped, skull back against the chair's headrest, resembling another piece of analytical equipment. "You're staying here, then?"

"I said I'd meet a friend."

"Cornelius?"

She blushed. "No. His sister."

"Aha." He drew in his breath and headed for the door. "The world's turned topsy-turvy!"

"That's only how you see it," said Una. Then she regretted the irony. She had no wish to hurt him.

---

## 4

*IS IT TRUE THAT THE SECRET OF S.S.P. HAD TURNED MEN INTO GODS AND CAN SHOW YOU HOW TO PROGRAM AND RECEIVE EVERYTHING YOU'VE EVER WANTED IN JUST SECONDS . . . INCLUDING RICHES, LUXURIOUS POSSESSIONS, POWER OVER OTHERS, AND EVEN A LONGER LIFE?*
*In a deal worth £180 million, Iran has selected the 'tracked' version of the Rapier low-level air defence system which is based on the FMC M548 armoured carrier. Iran already operates the standard Rapier version.*

Interavia

---

UNA AND CATHERINE were completely out of ammunition by the time they hit the IBM building. They were disturbed to find that the building had not been defended at all and suspected a trap. They proceeded warily across the campus, but it seemed the remaining students had fallen back to the great hall. The two women ducked into the low concrete entrance and ran along the corridor, bursting in on the computer room. The machine filled all available wall space on four sides. But it was dead. None of its indicators flickered, none of its lights glowed and its tapes no longer rotated.

"We've been done," said Catherine. She threw her carbine butt-first at a battleship-grey panel. It bounced back towards her so that she had to skip aside. It rattled across the floor. "This bugger isn't controlling anything. There's no power."

"I wonder why Maxime said she thought it was the centre of operations." Una lit a thin brown cigarette.

"Because she couldn't bear the idea of being in any way responsible herself," said Catherine spitefully. She patted at a blonde Marcel wave. "What a cock-up eh? What a bloody waste of time!"

"That's the trouble with computers," said Una. "They do confuse things."

"And take a lot of heat away from those who deserve to get it," said Catherine. She bent down wearily to pick up her M16. "Come on. Let's see if we can find any ammo outside."

"Wait," said Una. She opened her arms to her friend. "I feel so lonely suddenly, don't you?"

Catherine shook her head, but she came to Una. "Not here," she said.

---

## 5

### WILL YOUR JOB BE NEXT TO GO?

*Fixed armament on the General Dynamics F-16 consists of an internally mounted M61A1 Vulcan 20mm gun installed aft of the cockpit and avionics bays. External stores can be carried on nine stations: one central underfuselage, six underwing and two wingtip. A Pave Penny laser tracker pod hardpoint is also provided . . . A potential world market for the F-16 is seen as 4,800 aircraft; the conservative programme basis is put at 1,500. Based purely on the F-16 replacing the F-104. General Evans has said that there is a potential market for some 2,000 aircraft. (Almost 2,500 F-104s were built and over 2,200 of these were exported.)*

Interavia

---

CATHERINE SEEMED TO have settled down nicely so Una left her in Kiev and took the night train for Warsaw. From Warsaw she went to Dubrovnik, a roundabout route but the safest (if her instincts were to be trusted). Large

movements of men and equipment were taking place everywhere and she walked up the gangplank of the S.S. *Kao An* with a deep sense of relief. By the next morning they were making steam, heading for the less cluttered environments of Darwin and Sandakan. They had scarcely made it into the Timor Sea, however, before the ship was commandeered by a South Korean gunboat and Una and a selection of passengers were packed off back to the West with stamps on their passports forbidding them ever to

cross beyond Lat. 30 or Long. 40 again. Paranoia was settling in all over it seemed. Una had tried to make friends with one of the Korean officers, to find out what their complaint was. The man had struck her lightly across the mouth, refusing to speak English; he found that he had enjoyed hitting her and slapped her again until his commander had reprimanded him, not from any humane motive but, as Una interpreted it, because he would lose face.

Arriving in London, which had been 'cleaned up', she was subjected to an investigation into her movements over the past three years. Since she had begun to suffer from amnesia it was difficult for her to answer the questions but, knowing that they would be satisfied with any information so long as they could make it jell with their preconceptions, she invented a life-story for herself which was not only acceptable to them but suited her. She regretted that it was fictional.

Prinz Lobkowitz, the new Minister for Controls, heard that she was in England and sent an invitation for her to join him for dinner, but she was too frightened to accept. She headed for the cotton wool zone, eventually settling near Box Hill until one evening the telephone rang. Since it had never been connected at her request she saw this as a sign and returned to London and the Convent of the Poor Clares in Ladbroke Grove where a cell was held in readiness for this sort of emergency. She was convinced however that she was not going to escape. Her lovers were closing in on her.

She became desperate in her search for an ideal, a cause, a focus, but nothing presented itself to her. She refused to find what she wanted in an individual. She wanted, she said, something bigger. She regretted that her mind refused to manufacture fresh evidence for her researches.

Eventually, rather than face the more familiar dangers, she gave herself up to the nuns who had been begging to help her since her arrival.

---

# 6

## THE STRANGE CASE OF THE PANTY-CLAD COED AND THE NIGHT-RIDING MONSTER

*Financial restrictions are pushing Western aircraft development in one direction, while the East Bloc nations, spearheaded by the Soviet Union, are moving in another. The most remarkable point is that the latest Soviet aircraft display a sophistication that was almost unthinkable only a few years ago. During the 1950s and 1960s, the tendency was for all but the most specialised combat aircraft (e.g. reconnaissance and anti-submarine warfare) to be simple and robust, and produced in large numbers. The MiG-21, for example, was described by one Western analyst as a 'throw-away fighter', scarcely more than a piloted projectile.*

Interavia

---

SOMETHING WAS HAPPENING in the lower back section of the left-hand side of her brain. Memories of childhood disguised the deeper issues. She tried to trace the association. A flicker of hope. A few more cells began to die. She settled the expensive Koss headphones more comfortably over her ears and listened to the music with desperate concentration. Humour? Love? A sense of relish? The images of demolished streets and overgrown parks got in the way again. Perhaps if she adjusted the balance a fraction? She felt for the control, fingered it, moved it. Her face ached as she squeezed her eyes still tighter. All her heroes and heroines were dead. Those she had met had proved to be unworthy of what she had to give.

*. . . I swear the moon turned to fire red. The night I was born . . .*

She focussed on the appropriate section of the cortex. Drugs could produce a terrible self-consciousness, particularly when coupled with psychiatric research. The brain scanned the brain, scanned the brain.

Surely it must be possible to awaken sections of the mind just as one could sensitise areas of the body? She was right inside now. She slipped out. Her sense of yearning became even more painful. Inside again. Out. She increased the volume. Inside.

A question of proteins. They were being manufactured. But would they be the right ones?

The tempo of the drumbeats increased.

Inside.

The memories of childhood began to dim. Now she was sure something lay behind them. Deeper. She had isolated

the cells at any rate.
  The music stopped.
  She screamed.

## 7

### THE QUESTION WITHOUT AN ANSWER

*The RBS70 missile system has been designed to provide extreme
mobility and rapid deployment with a very short reaction time against
high-speed aircraft flying at the lowest possible altitudes. The
RBS70 missile system has recently been ordered by the Swedish
Army, in an order worth nearly SKr-500 million. First deliveries,
mostly of training equipment, will start in 1976, with series
production by 1977. Bofors is also looking at future developments,
including a possible nightfire version using electro-optical sensors for*

128

*target detection. At the moment the visibility limitation on the use of the weapon is the ability of the crew to see the target. The laser guidance system is able to provide guidance under any conditions in which the target is visible.*

Interavia

---

WITHIN THE SKULL the universe was at war.

Maxime and Catherine, Jerry and Lobkowitz stood on each side of the white hospital bed, their eyes fixed on the tragic face.

"She was looking for love," said Maxime.

"I loved her," said Jerry a little shiftily.

"So did I," said his sister.

"We all loved her," said Lobkowitz. "She was Life. She was Liberty. She was Hope."

"She was Future," said Jerry. "Fusion and fission, the glowing, rolling obsidian ranges of the post-war landscape." He sighed.

"But she was trying to love us, you see," continued Lobkowitz. "She wanted what we saw in her—she looked for the same things in us and could not find them. This is a good hospital. They will do what they can."

Maxime nodded. "Our people specialise in such complaints. *Tout cela vous honore/Lord Pierrot, mais encore?*"

Jerry glared a little resentfully at his rival.

"She thought she experienced it so many times," said Catherine, "but she was always disappointed. And yet she continued to seek that love, against all the odds."

"She loved it all," Maxime shrugged. "All of it."

"The data became confusing towards the end." Lobkowitz was sad.

"I could have simplified it." Jerry pouted. "Only nobody would let me." Then he laughed spontaneously. "Too much!"

And for a moment the electrodes protruding from Una's skull quivered in sympathy with the sounds from her mouth.

# CODA

## Harlequin Transformed

3/4   (A sort of carousel tune)


Destroyed by a comedy I did not devise
I've reached the limit of my changes
Repeating tricks solely for my eyes
Now, at last, my legend ages
And reveals the structure of my lies . . .


And my body alters as I watch
Black mask fades
My skin is pale
The colour leaves my costume
And I'm no longer Harlequin
—I am defeated from within


4/4


Say goodbye to Harlequin
Poor Pierrot now replaces him . . .


3/4


By a legend I sustained
Sardonic gaze and vicious brain
By mythology I maintained
The posture that I feigned
Inevitably my pose dissolved
Entropy has left me cold
And Harlequin is slain—
Again . . .


4/4 (rep. tune Every Gun)

Drip, drip, drip, drip
Here come's the rain


(Plink, plink, plink, plink—plucked on violin) *Abrupt End.*

## Pierrot and Columbine's Song of Reconciliation

Divided I love you
And united become you
Columbine, Columbine
We are one at last

        Rejecting all armour
        Thus we are conquered
        Conquered, we vanquish
        All that we fear

Pierrot and Columbine
(Harlequin with them)
Conquered, we vanquished
All that we feared . . .

*(This leads into the tune of the Entropy Tango, acting as an introduction for the reprise, which is up-tempo, cheerful . . .)*

## The Entropy Tango (Reprise—The Ensemble)

For a while at least it's all right
We're safe from Chaos and Old Night
The Cold of Space won't chill our veins
—We have danced the Entropy Tango . . .

So we'll love, love, love
One another like two doves . . .
And we'll hug, hug, hug
We can never have enough . . .
The power of love has won this throw
—We have danced the Entropy Tango . . .

And it's kiss, kiss, kiss
Fear and hate we have dismissed
And it's wish, wish, wish . . .
For a better world than this . . .
So say goodbye to pain and woe
—And we'll stop the Entropy Tango . . .

133

# 5. HARLEQUIN'S LAMENT

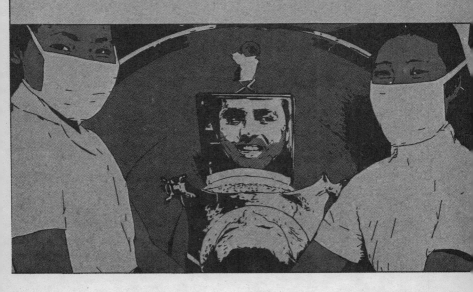

*This is the personal flag of the Sovereign, and a symbol of the tie which unites under one monarch the British Dominions throughout the world. The three golden lions represent England, the red lion rampant Scotland, while the golden harp stands for Ireland—the three states from which the Empire grew. Royal personages have the right to fly royal standards, members of the Royal Family having their particular standards. This flag should only be hoisted when H.M. the King is actually present, and ought never to be used for purposes of decoration.*

*In the Royal Navy, by special privilege, the King's health is always drunk sitting.*

Flags of the Empire, No. 1, issued by W.D. & H.O. Wills,
c. 1924

---

AT SUNSET, WHEN the beggars in Chowringhee settled themselves into doorways for the night and the kites and vultures on the lamp-posts and telephone poles roosted, reconciled that they must wait for a fresh day to bring them their share of death and garbage, Mrs Persson would climb into her rickshaw and let the ageless coolie, in his turban and his loincloth, run with her to the Empire where she was starring as Diana Hunt in the musical comedy *Wonderful Woman*. She played a Greek goddess transported to 1930 (with hilarious misunderstandings) who eventually gives up all her powers to marry the hero and become an ordinary housewife. Una considered the role ideal. It was the sensation of Calcutta.

Through the mobs of cyclists, pedestrians, rickshaws; past the trams, bullock carts, limousines, trucks, taxis, buses which blared and flared in the twilight, darted Una and her coolie, until at last they reached the marble face of the Empire (with her name in electric lights above its Graecian portico) round to the stage entrance, a little bit late as usual. Una got out and the rickshaw was off (she paid it weekly) and she, in silks and chiffon, in her Reynolds hat and veil, briskly went through nodding to the

Bengali stage-door keeper, who smiled and nodded at her. He was trusted by the management. He was one of the very few natives they employed at present. So many young Bengalis were anarchists and might be expected to attack the theatre.

Una got to her dressing room and became suddenly wary, for the door was open and voices emerged. She recomposed herself and entered. She vaguely recalled the couple who waited for her—the fat clergyman with his hat in his fingers, the thin bluestocking in pale linen. Her dresser began to speak rapidly in her lilting English. Una smiled. "It's all right, Ranee. Bishop Beesley and—?

"I'm Miss Brunner. We met, I believe, at Mrs Brightsett's garden party. Last week."

"Oh, yes. And I promised you tickets!"

"No," said Bishop Beesley. "We are from the local Moral Rearmament Committee."

"This play is objectionable? Surely not."

"The play is fine. There's one scene, that's all." Bishop Beesley brightened as Ranee offered him some of Una's Turkish Delight.

"Which one?"

"The . . ." he mumbled the confection, ". . . second act. Scene one."

"Where I have my first drink?"

"Yes." Miss Brunner spoke significantly.

"The audience love it. It's the funniest."

"It's very good." Miss Brunner seemed baffled. "But we wondered if you could accommodate us. Accommodate the residents of the city, really. Anywhere else, I'm sure it would not be important—but there are Bengalis in the audience, and Anglo-Indians and so on, as well as English people."

"Yes."

"And we feel the scene could—" Bishop Beesley wiped sugary lips "—corrupt some of them."

"Because of me getting tipsy? I would have thought there was a moral there—not to drink."

"You could see it as that," Miss Brunner agreed, "but when it is combined with your costume . . ."

"A bit flimsy?"

"Exactly," said Bishop Beesley in relief.

"And the language," said Miss Brunner. "I mean— what you say."

"What do I say?"

"Something about crime and anarchy?"

"Ah, yes: Here's to crime and here's to anarchy! I'm showing my frustration. I come round in the end."

"Not the best-chosen line, given the current political climate."

"I don't know anything about politics," Una told them.

Ranee brought over some tea. "Tea?" added Una.

139

"Thank you. Even you, Mrs Persson," continued the bishop, "must realise there have been bombings of white people almost daily. In the name of the anarchist cause." He unrolled a copy of *The Englishman* and pointed out its headline: ANARCHY: A CHALLENGE TO THE EMPIRE. "It's in the leading article. And you should read the Bengali papers. Full of such stuff."

"What stuff?" asked Una.

"Anarchy," said Miss Brunner, lifting her cup. "They get it all from France, I believe."

"Aha," said Una. She sat down at her mirror and looked at her face. She gave herself a wink. "Well, I'll bear it in mind, of course. Thanks for pointing the problem out."

"You'll change your lines? And your costume?"

"I'll certainly give it some thought," Una promised.

## 2

*What man that sees the eur-whirling wheele*
*Of Change, the which all mortall things doth sway,*
*But that therby doth find, & plainly feele,*
*How MUTABILITY in them doth play*
*Her cruell sports, to many mens decay?*
*Which that to all may better yet appear,*
*I will rehearse that whylome I heard say,*
*How she at first her selfe began to reare,*
*Gainst all the Gods, and th'empire fought from them to beare.*

Spenser, The Fairie Queene, 7. vi. 1.

AS THE TRAIN pulled out of Odessa, leaving the warmth and the ocean behind, Una swayed on her feet, attempting to freshen her face in the mirror above the opposite seats. Her lipstick dropped from her hand and fell onto green plush. She said: "Damn!" and bent to look for it just as the compartment door opened and a man holding a carpet-bag entered and raised his straw hat. He wore rimless glasses and had the kind of goatee beard which hid nothing of his face, added no character and was perhaps a badge to make it clear that he was an intellectual. The casual Norfolk, the unpressed trousers, the peasant shirt, all proclaimed his chosen role and, of course, he addressed her in French rather than Russian. "Excusez moi, mademoiselle."

Una had recognised him. It was the old butcher himself. He couldn't see past her heavy make-up.

"Bronstein!" she laughed. "Are you back in favour?"

He relaxed, at the same time displaying his embarrassment. "It's you, comrade. Dressed up like a bourgeois whore. What are you doing? Going all the way?"

"Hoping to. Kiev?"

"I change there. I don't like this part of the world much. The people are lazy. Too rich, all of them."

"All?"

"By my standards. What have you been up to?" He offered her a Sobranie which she accepted because she liked the feel of the gold tip on her mouth.

"I've been resting," she said. "I'm too tired, darling."

"And why are you in Russia?"

"I'm not in Russia. I'm in Ukrainia."

"You have a pass?" He pulled a card from his pocket. He seemed to be proud of the distinction. "Like this? It's a special pass. Everyone must help me."

"You're not posing as an anarchist now!"

"What's the difference? We're all socialists. I shall represent Kiev in Moscow and resume my position as head of the Bureau. In time." He opened his bag and took out a large notebook. "I have agreed to put the South Russian case."

"They don't need it put. They're strong—and rich. You said so yourself." The train began to move faster. They were in Odessa's new garden suburbs. The light was perfect. Una stared out of the window, back at the misty sea with all its ships, inland at the green steppe ahead. "You've conned them. You'll use their strength to help you get your job back! You cunning old bastard."

Trotski sniffed. "I have a case to put. I must have an effective power-base if I am to put it properly."

"And Stalin?"

Trotski pursed his lips and smiled. "Didn't you know? He's dead."

"I'll never understand politics." Una looked out at golden fields and saw horsemen riding along the nearby white road. They were racing the train, waving their caps as they spurred their ponies. She was reminded of the old days, of Makhno and his riders. She waved back. They were past. She returned her attention to Trotski. "Maybe that's why I find them so eternally appealing."

He leaned forward and put a familiar hand on her knee. "Where have you been for the past five years? This time I want the truth.'' He attempted joviality.

"You'll have it," she said. "But you'll never appreciate it."

"Don't be mysterious." He leaned back and picked up his book. He took a fountain pen from his inside pocket. "It irritates me."

"I can't be anything else. I'm Una. I'm the truth. Eh?"

"You're the very antithesis. You've gone back to acting, I see."

"I had. But I've given it up again. I'm on my way to see a friend in Kiev."

"Makhno, that hooligan?"

"No. Quite another hooligan. He's not fond of you."

"Few are," he said smugly. "Who is it?"

"Jerry."

"Cornelius. Bah! He's no threat at all. Except to himself. I thought he was liquidated. Or in a coma or something."

"It's not his turn."

He removed his glasses. The gesture was meant as a warning signal. He drew heavily on his cigarette as he leaned forward. "Stop it! Una!" He wagged his finger. He was pretending to joke.

Una felt the familiar terror. She drew in a breath and was defiant. It was just what she had needed.

---

## 3

### THE RIVER

*It is during the Diwali festival, when the darkest night in October is illumined by myriad bonfires, each symbolising a life sacrificed in the conflict between good and evil, that the girl, Harriet, falls in love with a young captain, lamed in the First World War. Lacking beauty, she hopes to win his heart by writing a poem for him about the legendary Radha, whose love for the god Krishna made her a goddess . . . In India all rivers—symbols of Eternity—are sacred . . .*
ARTICLE: Picture Post, 1 March 1952

---

THE GOLDEN GATE BRIDGE SAGGED AND SQUEALED AS THE EXPLOSIVE TOOK IT OUT.

BEHIND THEM, THE Golden Gate Bridge sagged and squealed as the explosive took it out. It was dawn. There were fires all over San Francisco, particularly in the suburbs. From the harbour the pirate ships continued to shell the city. They were retreating now. On the bridge of the submarine liner *Seahorse* Una, her face blackened by smoke, her hand on the butt of her holstered revolver, looked at their hostages—almost all young men and women—totting up their value in her head. They would be ransomed.

The fleet, mainly a mixture of commercial and naval submarines stolen from half the countries in the world, had arrived at midnight, surfacing in the bay to begin its attack. It had fought off the few defending airships, and, in the time gained while Washington hesitated, had been able to loot the city of most of what they had come for.

Makhno, in a long leather coat and riding britches, an M60 in his left hand, joined her on the bridge. His men were hauling boxes aboard. "There it is, Una. All the gold of Sacramento."

She was a little dismayed at his tone. "You sound like a bandit."

"Don't be moralistic now you've had your fun. There's something Victorian about you, Una. Always washing your hands. I am a successful bandit!" He touched her arm gently. He was very old. The white hair was growing thin. His movements, however, were those of a ballet dancer—imitating youth from training and habit.

He went below, making some noise, and greeted the Pole, Captain Korzeniowski, who had inadvertently inspired this raid with his tales of gold and who had commanded the *Seahorse* ('For safety and comfort in troubled times, these luxurious hotels of the deep will get you where you want to go in the condition you'd wish to arrive!') before Makhno had requisitioned her. Korzeniowski was contemptuous. "How many hundreds of innocents has your raid destroyed?"

"There are no innocents in this struggle." Makhno spoke automatically and Una felt sad. The years had at last succeeded in coarsening him. It had been almost inevitable. She leaned down towards where the hostages still stood watching the gold being lowered into the special hatches. "Let them go. Give them boats." She told the guards. She would not take any more responsibility.

In a dinghy coming alongside from their own wrecked sub, Shakey Mo and Jerry called out to her. They were filthy and jubilant. Cornelius at least was drunk. It was always hard to tell with Mo what sort of condition he was in.

"Mrs P." Jerry raised a bottle of wine in a salute. He began to get up but the rocking boat made him sit down again. "Ready to leave when you are!"

"Not long now," she said. She searched the sky for dawn, but the flames obscured it.

"This is what I call effective political action," said Mo. "We need our course. We had the chart on the bridge when that bloody destroyer got us. Dropped a fucking great torpedo, didn't it."

She had seen them leap into the sea just before the destroyer had, in turn, been blown out of the sky.

Could she hear screaming from the city? Smoke clogged her nostrils, stung her eyes. The suburbs were on fire, now. Many wooden houses were burning and they sweetened the otherwise acrid air.

Mo scrambled over the rail. "Better than any earthquake," he said. "Better than any Indian raid. Where are we headed? My guess was Mexico."

"You're not far out," said Una. Mo clinked and looked embarrassed. "What have you got this time?" she asked.

"Nothing much." His grin was sheepish. He reached into one of his several sacks and pulled out a coin. "Pieces of eight. Doubloons. And that . . ."

"Where on earth did you get them?"

"The museum. I always hit the museum first. You know me. An incurable bloody romantic. I love old things."

She felt affection for him. More than she felt at that moment for the others.

"This did used to be called the Barbary Coast," he said defensively.

"Wasn't that in Africa somewhere?"

"No," he said. "You're thinking of the Mountains of the Moon." He vanished into the liner's enormous hull.

Una saw that Jerry was helping some of the girls into the boat he had abandoned. He looked as harmless as they did. He was being very gentle with them. She drew a deep breath and controlled her tears.

"It all seems a bit self-indulgent, really," she said.

Fisherman's Wharf exploded suddenly and she was blinded.

# 4

## HOOLIGANISM ON SOCCER TERRACES
### "HARMLESS RITUAL"

*Soccer hooliganism provides a harmless outlet for aggression which could take more violent forms, says an Oxford psychologist in a book published today. Battles between rival groups on soccer terraces are an artificial form of violence rather than the real thing, and few people really get hurt, says Mr Peter Marsh, of the Oxford University Department of Experimental Psychology. In 'Aggro: the Illusion of Violence,' he appeals to people to learn to live with 'aggro'—fights between rival gangs of youths at football matches, dance halls and public houses—rather than trying to stamp it out. 'By trying to eradicate aggro we end up with something far more sinister. Instead of social violence we get non-social violence that manifests itself in random, gratuitous injury . . . By learning to live with aggro . . . we begin to see that illusions of violence are much preferable to the very real violence which maims and kills . . .' Mr Marsh sees 'Aggro' between rival gangs as an equivalent of tribal warfare in less developed societies.*

Daily Telegraph, 20 July 1978

---

ALTHOUGH THE HOSPITAL was virtually silent, it seemed to Una that there was a threat in the air. She tried to move her eyes a little further than they would comfortably go. The metal cage keeping her head in position (she had a broken neck) allowed her no flexibility. Major Nye was still there, holding her hand. He was half asleep, his gaze fixed on the opposite bed. He attempted to carry on the conversation where it had stopped, five minutes before. "Yes," he said. "It's the vermin."

"Rats?"

"Mainly."

"Models, metaphors—even examples, I suppose." Una was glad that they had taken the screen away and she could see at least part of the ward with its privileged beds. The hospital was run by nuns and was private. There was no vermin here to speak of.

147

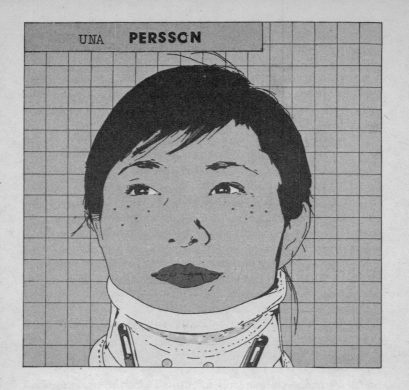

UNA **PERSSON**

"I see what you mean." He smiled. "You're too imaginative."

"I live in a world of poetry," she said. "Or rather, of poetic images. Everything seems significant to me. Everything has meaning. It's what gets me into trouble. And I never listen. I only watch."

He patted her hand.

She heard very soft sounds and thought at first that she was listening to his hand on hers, but they were footfalls. At the end of the bed stood Prinz Lobkowitz. "They haven't moved you yet?"

"Not yet." Major Nye answered for her. He got up and brought a chair to place next to his own. "Sit down, old boy. You look very tired.''

Lobkowitz's back was stooped. His grey hair fell over his face. The skin of his face had become baggy with care. Una felt frustrated. She wished she could be of help.

''Makhno?'' she said.

''Dead. The Americans caught him at last. He was electrocuted three days ago. In Oregon, I believe.''

''The Californians gave him up.''

''Californians are like Greeks. They talk themselves into things and then they talk themselves out of them again. It must be the sunshine. No, he's buried in some Portland cemetery. Shall I get you the details?''

''It's pointless,'' she said. ''I'll be in this thing for six months.''

''Yes.''

''He made a name for himself, at least,'' said Major Nye. ''There's no one in the world hasn't heard of Nestor Makhno. He's a hero and a martyr in six continents. And his example lives on.'' He was trying to console her, but he could not fail to register a little disapproval. She gripped his wrist.

''Don't worry,'' she said. ''It's a victory for your sort of rationalism, major.''

''I've never much cared for my sort of rationalism. Not in isolation, anyway. I see myself as a balancing force—not as a positive one. Makhno represented all I envied. It was the same sort of balance which controlled the Empire for so long—we all admired the Bengalis, you know. And the Pathans. It's a terrible sort of paternalism, I suppose, but it had certain simple virtues.''

''Are you sure there are such things as simple virtues?'' Prinz Lobkowitz's accent had grown a shade stronger. ''I would say that only vice was simple.''

Major Nye hadn't followed him. ''You sound as if you've come to preach the last rites,'' he said. ''I don't think you'd make a very good clergyman, Prinz.''

''Oh, I'm not so sure!'' He strove for levity and failed miserably. ''A couple of hundred years or so ago I could have filled the role you see as your own, major. A temporiser. Mm?''

''Church and State stuff. There's a fair bit to be said for the ideas of the middle-ages. We've complicated them rather, haven't we, without improving on them.''

''I wouldn't say that,'' said Una. She attempted to move and failed. The harness was firm.

''We're taking you by airship to the coast,'' said Prinz Lobkowitz. ''And then, perhaps when you're whole again, a cruise.''

''I might have had enough of cruises.''

''We'll see.''

''Do you good,'' said Major Nye with weary mindlessness.

''I'll happily take over.'' Prinz Lobkowitz smiled at his old friend. ''You could do with some shut-eye, eh?''

''About as much as you.'' Major Nye appreciated the thought. ''But I haven't any travelling in the morning. I'll carry on here.''

''You should both rest.'' Una hoped they would not take her seriously. She was terrified of being left in the hospital. She needed one of them there at least, to comfort her.

''Well,'' said Major Nye, ''perhaps you're right. Will you sleep now, Una?''

''Oh, yes. Of course.''

They rose; two tired ghosts. ''Goodbye.''

*Buf if he sees a sad face staring through the glamour of light, the face of a girl who is thinking of a lover who comes no more to her Christmas parties, of an old mother whose children have gone about their business in the world, Pierrot will go on tiptoe to them, and lay a hand lightly on their shoulders, and say, 'It is not good to remember too much. Play the game of life. I have suffered too; but listen to my laughter on this Christmas night. Come, play the fool with me! Why, there is little Columbine who flouted me three hundred years ago! Bless her sweet heart; I will steal a kiss tonight.'*
THE SPIRIT OF PIERROT by Phillip Gibbs, The Graphic, 27 November 1911

———————————————————————

THE WHITE STEAM-yacht moved slowly through the drifts of ice. Steam curled from her deck as she gave her heat to the Arctic. The blue sky was like thin ice enclosing them. It was as if they sailed through the semi-fluid remains of some frozen confection, under glass. This was no place, thought Una as she pulled her huge white furs around her, for *The Teddy Bear*. It was no place for her, for that matter. She coughed and more heat escaped her to be absorbed by that unambiguous continent. The yacht bumped against a few small floes and the engines stalled for a second, then started up again, firmly pushing the ship on, heading closer and closer to the Pole.

From below came the sound of a piano, thin and brittle, and the applause of the guests. They had already had their turkey. They had opened their presents. Now the party was to begin with an entertainment.

Una turned from the tranquility of endless ice and made her way to the louvred door which would lead her down. The ship, though strengthened in her hull, had been designed for warm weather cruising.

In the saloon the audience had gathered. "All our old chums," as Bishop Beesley had said. He had handed over control of the ship only after he had been locked up for an afternoon without sweets. He was in the front row now, with a plate of cake and candy on his knees. Miss Brunner, wearing a paper hat on her violent red hair, sat next to him. She held a tiny piece of marzipan between the finger and thumb of her left hand. Her right hand rested against Maxime. The bishop's blonde daughter, Mitzi, glared at them from the other side of her corpulent dad.

Una removed her coat and revealed herself as Harlequin. She put on her mask and her cap. She bowed and was cheered. Mrs Cornelius, behind the bishop, blew a friendly raspberry. Major Nye began to vamp a 4/4 tango. He looked a little incongruous in his clown costume. Columbine (played by Catherine) curtsyed on the tiny stage. Behind her, wistful as ever, stood Pierrot, pretending to play a guitar.

The audience began to clap in time to the music, so loudly that the words of the song could not be heard at all.

Outside, the ice grew thicker and it seemed it must soon stop the ship completely. The steam from the white decks was growing denser, almost hiding her from view, as the passengers put their hearts and souls into their enjoyment of the show.

A little faint music found an echo in the distant mountains; the ancient ice.

If it was to be a farewell performance, none of the actors had yet guessed. They sang louder and louder above the steady drumming of the applause, which took on the nature of a gigantic heartbeat. They sang as loud as they could. They sang with gusto. They sang for all the world.


### THE END

## Also by Michael Moorcock

**The Cornelius Chronicles**
*The Final Programme*
*A Cure for Cancer*
*The English Assassin*
*The Condition of Muzak*
*The Lives and Times of Jerry Cornelius*
*The Aventures of Una Persson and Catherine Cornelius in the Twentieth Century*
*The Great Rock and Roll Swindle*
*The Entropy Tango*

**The Dancers at the End of Time**
*The Hollow Lands*
*An Alien Heat*
*The End of All Songs*
*Legends from the End of Time*
*The Transformation of Miss Mavis Ming [Return of the Fireclown]*

**Hawkmoon: The History of the Runestaff**
*The Jewel in the Skull*
*The Mad God's Amulet*
*The Sword of the Dawn*
*The Runestaff*

**Hawkmoon: The Chronicles of Castle Brass**
*Count Brass*
*The Champion of Garathorm* *
*The Quest for Tanelorn* *

**Erekosë**
*The External Champion*
*Phoenix in Obsidian*
*The Champion of Garathorm* *
*The Quest for Tanelorn* *

*interconnected series

**Elric Series**
*Elric of Melnibone*
*The Sailor on the Seas of Fate*
*The Sleeping Sorceress*
*The Stealer of Souls*
*Stormbringer*
*Elric at the End of Time*

**The Books of Corum**
*The Knight of the Swords*
*The Queen of the Swords*
*The King of the Swords*
*The Bull and the Spear*
*The Oak and the Ram*
*The Sword and the Stallion*

**Other titles**
*The City of the Beast*
*The Lord of the Spiders*
*The Masters of the Pit*
*The Warlord of the Air*
*The Land Leviathan*
*The Steel Tsar*
*The Winds of Limbo*
*Behold the Man*
*Breakfast in the Ruins*
*The Blood-Red Game*
*The Black Corridor*
*The Chinese Agent*
*The Russian Intelligence*
*The Distant Suns*
*The Rituals of Infinity*
*The Shores of Death*
*Sojan the Swordsman* (juvenile)
*The Golden Barge*
*Gloriana [or, The Unfulfill'd Queene, A Romance]*
*The Time Dweller* (short stories)
*Moorcock's Book of Martyrs* (short stories)
*Heroic Dreams* (non-fiction)
*The War Hound and the World's Pain*
*My Experiences in the Third World War*
*Byzantium Endures*